BOX
100

BOX 100

Frank Leonard

1817

HARPER & ROW, PUBLISHERS

New York   Evanston   San Francisco   London

A JOAN KAHN–HARPER NOVEL OF SUSPENSE

FIRST EDITION

STANDARD BOOK NUMBER: 06–012583–7

LIBRARY OF CONGRESS CATALOG CARD NUMBER: 70–175154

To Brenda
To Papo
To Jill
and her parents
and to all the others

BOX
100

one

IT WAS NINE-THIRTY in the morning, and I was sitting alone in the shabby little office of the Box 100 section of the New York City Department of Investigation. I was supposed to begin work as a special investigator and I was waiting for someone to get there and explain the job to me. At age forty-six I was starting what I calculated to be my twenty-seventh job and my first as a gumshoe.

Box 100 had been set up by the previous mayor. Any citizen could write in to Box 100 with a complaint about wrongdoing in city government. While I waited I read some of the letters that were lying around the office.

Dear Box 100. The woman in the next room just got out of a Mental Hospital. She goes out in the hall in her unerwear. She has a lot of moles on her back. She talks to her self. I can hear her through my wall. Shes making me crazy. I complained to the presink but they wont do nothing. Im going cut her damn eyes out. Joseph Castori, 205 West 71st Street, New York.

I put the letter down and picked up another.

Box 100, Alfred O' Reilly drives a truck for the Sanitation Department, Long Island City depot. Every truck is suppose to pick up so many tons of trash a day then go to the dump and unload. A supervisor at the dump weighs the truck to make sure it's full. Alfred just drives to an empty lot near the midtown tunnel and they fill up with stones and old cement blocks so their truck will seem full and then they sit around and drink beer and read the *Daily News* for the rest of the day. Some days they drive to the dump and only pertend to unload so the next day they don't even have to pick up any stones. You can reconize Alfred because he is bald and has Hazel eyes and a gold cap on his left front tooth. He is 39 years old and single. His badge number is 6656. Yours truly, a loyal citizen.

I picked up a third letter.

Dear Box Hundered, A woman in this bilding name Jones pretend to lose her Welfare Check and they give her another one and then she cash both Checks She have a Boy Frend live with her. I am Ophelia Harm, 119 Herzl Street, Brooklyn.

Next was a square envelope addressed to "Major Wagner, Box 100." Wagner had not been mayor for years. Inside the envelope was a flowery birthday card signed "A frend."

As I put the card down the office door opened and in stepped a freckle-faced man with bright-red curly hair. He wore a wrinkled tan wash-and-wear suit and a Hawaiian-style pink, orange, red and purple flowered shirt with the first three buttons open, revealing more freckles and curly red hair on his chest.

"Hi," he said. "You the new guy?"

"Yes. Ross Franklin."

"Pat McCann," said the man, sticking out his hand, which I shook. "That idiot here yet?" he asked, gesturing with his head toward the door of an inner office.

"No."

"Good," he said. "I can give you some of the facts before he gets here." He sat down in his swivel chair, opened his middle right-hand drawer, propped up his feet and tilted back. "If we're lucky we only get a few of these fuckin' letters a day," he said. "Sometimes we don't get any. Then we work on the backlog. That's the backlog file." He gestured with his head toward a file cabinet marked "Confidential."

"The only time we get a lot of letters is when Box 100 is mentioned in the newspapers—knock wood." McCann rapped the gray plastic top of his desk with his knuckles.

"We had it made the last few months until that asshole Cooper"—again the gesture toward the inner office—"wrote an article about Box 100 for a civil service newspaper. The next week we got two hundred letters.

"Most of the backlog goes back to the first part of 1969, when somebody wrote in to Box 100 from the Department of Purchase and blew the whistle on a huge black market operation they had going over there. Box 100 was in and out of the papers for months. Fifteen guys got indicted. Everybody and his brother began to write in to us. One dumb bastard wrote in and confessed to stealing seventy-five dollars' worth of tokens from his job with the Transit Authority. He said he was sending back thirty-five dollars in cash along with his letter and would send the rest later. The letter was all ripped up and taped back together when it got here and there was no money in it. I guess the mailman intercepted it. They fired the guy from the Transit Authority. A guy that stupid shouldn't be driving a bus anyway.

"We even got a letter from Hoboken, New Jersey, with a snapshot of a policeman in bed with a half-naked woman."

McCann took off his jacket. Underneath he was wearing a pistol in a shoulder holster. He unstrapped it and laid it in his "Out" box.

"You oughta get yourself one of these," he advised. "You can never tell what kind of a creep is gonna come up to you in the subway. The other day a kid without any fingers was shaking his hand in my face."

He looked at the letters I had been reading. "Most of this crap we just send to the city department that handles that kind of problem. This one about the nut from the mental hospital we'll send to police headquarters."

"Why?" I said.

"Because it's a complaint about the precinct. Or we could send it to the Department of Hospitals. Cooper goes over it all

3

again anyway, so if I put down 'Police' he'll change it to 'Hospitals' anyway. And if I put down 'Hospitals' he'll change it to 'Police.' Now this one about Sanitation Cooper will probably want to look into himself because there might be something to it. Every letter that has a return address, that dumb broad they call a secretary"—and he gestured with his head toward the empty desk across from his own—"sends a form letter of acknowledgment."

As if on cue, the secretary came into the office. She was a tall, skinny, forty-year-old woman with a long, thin nose and beautiful radiant blue eyes with long lashes. Her arms were full of library and paperback books, packages, a huge purse and a small folding umbrella. Before she got to her desk, a library book slipped out of her arms to the floor, then a paperback book, then a package, then the umbrella. They fell on the floor near McCann, but he didn't move. As she reached her desk she opened her arms and let the rest of the books and packages fall onto it with a clatter.

"See what I mean?" said McCann. "That's her."

"Hello," I said.

She smiled shyly but didn't look up. She began to retrieve the packages. Still looking down, she spoke to McCann. "Good morning, Mr. McCann," she said, and blushed deeply.

"Oh, Christ," said McCann. He ignored her and picked up the birthday card addressed to "Major Wagner." "Stupid asshole," he said. He picked up a mimeographed form that listed every city agency and checked "Miscellaneous," the last line on the form. Then he stapled the card to the form and threw it into my "Out" box.

"What happens to that one?" I asked.

"First Cooper reads it. Then he sends the 'Miscellaneous' to his boss, Vanderbilt, another asshole. Vanderbilt checks to make sure it really should be in the 'Miscellaneous' category and then he okays it for the 'Case Closed' category and it gets filed."

4

He picked up another letter from my desk, tore it open and read it aloud, giving extra emphasis to the misspelled words:

"We have rats, *roach,* broken windows, filthy halls, the *junks* use the empty apartments, Jo-Jo lives under, he's blind, can't see eats food with *roach* in it The city inspector came yesterday and didn't write anything in his book. I think the landlord gives money. Please *held us.* God bless you We tried everything else I am 80. I know you will *held.* Very truly yours. Temperance Charity, 109 West 116 Street."

"Stupid old bag," said McCann. "Lives in Harlem and doesn't even know how to spell 'junkie.'"

The secretary had been peeping shyly and admiringly at McCann over the top of some papers. "It's j-u-n-k-i-e, right, Mr. McCann?" she asked.

McCann ignored her and continued to talk to me about the letter. "I can use this. This'll be my first investigation for this week. Cooper wants us to investigate at least two of these letters a week so we can put it on our monthly report. Let's see . . . this is Tuesday . . . I'll dictate my report on this one now and put Thursday's date on it. Thursday I got an eleven A.M. date with a ten-dollar chippie—some of the chippies that work in offices around here have a hustle going on Canal Street. They pick up an extra ten or twenty dollars a day turning tricks on their lunch hours. They have it set up just like a little office."

McCann gave an imitation of their officelike efficiency: " 'Whom shall I say is calling? . . . Do you have an appointment? . . . Then I'll have to check and see if Miss Jones can squeeze you in between her eleven-thirty and her twelve-o'clock.' " McCann grinned. "They even hire a full-time receptionist. She's the best-looking broad there and she won't turn tricks."

McCann took Temperance Charity's letter back to his desk, put a little green disk on the recording machine and

5

began to dictate in a very professional, detectivelike voice.

"Thursday, comma, July 13, period. This is Special Investigator Patrick McCann dictating on Charity, comma, Temperance, comma, 109 West 116 Street, period."

The secretary had whipped two sheets of paper into her typewriter and was typing McCann's report as he dictated it, without waiting to get the little green record. She was a lightning-fast typist, and getting McCann's words onto paper in an instant seemed to please her. She watched him attentively and waited for each phrase.

"Paragraph," said McCann. The secretary was ahead of him. She had already thrown the typewriter carriage and spaced for the paragraph. "On the above date, comma, we visited the above complainant, comma, and made a thorough investigation, comma, of the allegations, comma, contained in her letter, period." He dictated the word "comma" as though it added an elegant flourish to his style.

"Her information, comma, proved to be inconclusive, period. No leads were developed, comma, which could be pursued, comma, further, period. End of report."

The secretary finished typing and whisked the paper out of her typewriter and into her middle desk drawer.

"Sign it 'Patrick McCann, Special Investigator,'" said McCann. She obviously had figured that out and typed it in already. McCann took the little green record off the machine and went over and dropped it on the secretary's desk.

"That's a standard investigation report," said McCann to me. "You'll get the hang of it. If it's anything serious, Cooper handles it. He digs a little and if he finds something he turns it over to senior investigators—a bunch of young wise guys just out of law school. We shovel the shit, they get the glory."

The office door opened again and an unsmiling little man entered. His mustache was little more than a few strands of almost invisible pinkish-blond hair on his upper lip. He wore a shiny old dark-blue pair of pants and the shiny dark-blue jacket of a slightly different-colored suit. Through his white Orlon wash-and-wear shirt you could see an undershirt with a small hole in it. In the middle of his nondescript black-and-blue striped necktie was a tiny piece of scrambled egg.

"Good morning, Mr. Cooper," said McCann.

"Good morning," said Cooper.

"Good morning," I said, "I'm Ross Franklin."

"Ross Franklin?" he asked, frowning as if my presence was adding more complexity to his morning than he was capable of dealing with. I usually take an instant dislike to people who hear a simple statement like "I'm Ross Franklin" and hand it back to you as a question. I decided to begin again as if he hadn't heard me.

"Good morning," I repeated. "I'm Ross Franklin."

"I think we got a letter about you," he said.

"You think you got a letter about me?" I said, giving him back some of his own medicine.

"Yeah. You're the new guy."

"I am?" I was starting to share McCann's opinion that the man was an asshole.

Cooper frowned and looked at me a little more carefully. "Pick out a letter to investigate," he said. "Use your own judgment. McCann will fill you in on the details." He picked up the letters I had been reading and leafed through them. "Here's a good one," he said, pulling out the one on welfare checks. "Investigate this one. I'll look into the one on Sanitation myself." Cooper turned to the secretary. "Give him the key to his desk, Laura."

He entered his inner office and closed the door. A moment later a cheap transistor radio was playing rock-and-roll music. I unlocked my desk and began to look through the drawers. In the middle right-hand one were six old *Playboy* magazines.

"Not bad," I said to McCann.

"Yeah, that was Herzog's desk," he said.

Herzog had either been a pinup fan or a suppressed sadist or both: the insides of the magazines had been shredded with a razor blade, either to remove pictures of naked girls or to hack them to bits. You couldn't be sure. On one page the portion of a naked girl from the middle of the nipples down had been sliced out; just the head and the top of the breasts remained.

The middle left-hand drawer contained an interoffice envelope with a freshly laundered white shirt in it. I checked the collar size. Sixteen and a half. It would fit. I put it in the $2.99 imitation-leather plastic briefcase I had bought in preparation for my new job.

In my experience, give or take a few exceptions, people only stole when they had the opportunity and only refrained from stealing when they didn't. In the fifties I had spent some time among a band of social workers in Arizona and every one of them admitted that he cheated on his income tax return. They rationalized it as a protest against Truman but continued the practice under Eisenhower.

The bottom left-hand drawer was crammed full of unopened letters to Box 100. Most of them had postmarks at least two months old. Lying in the middle of the letters like a crimson egg in a paper nest was a pint bottle of cheap burgundy. I opened it and took a swallow.

"Not bad for cheap burgundy," I said.

"I never touch anything but Fresca," said McCann.

Suddenly I had a taste for something better and decided to go out and see what the neighborhood offered in the way of liquor stores. I claim I'm merely a society drinker: I drink in order to stand society. Eleven months out of the year I drink a bottle or two of good wine a day. It's never interfered with my holding down a job; it's what made most of the jobs bearable. During the twelfth month I don't touch a drop, to prove I'm not an alcoholic. (In recent years, sometimes twelve months go by so fast that the year is over before I've been able to make up my mind which month to give up the wine.)

"Can I get you anything outside?" I asked McCann and the secretary. She shook her head.

"Fresca," said McCann. "In a can."

When I reached the elevator, a young man with blue shoes, bright purple pants and a green shirt was standing there. His pupils were enormously dilated. He was holding a brand-new electric typewriter with the cord dragging on the floor. I suspected he was stealing the typewriter but I couldn't be sure.

Across from us, facing the elevator, a buxom somewhat elderly receptionist sat behind a desk and a pimply-faced young guard in a dark-green uniform was leaning on the desk and looking down her low-cut blouse. If he wasn't concerned about the man with the typewriter, I decided I needn't be either. The man with the typewriter and I rode down in the elevator together.

Coming back ten minutes later with some good burgundy, a corkscrew, two five-and-ten wineglasses and a can of Fresca, I found the guard and the receptionist in almost exactly the same positions. As I went down the hall toward the Box 100 office I saw the young man with the purple pants and green shirt emerge from an office with another electric typewriter in his arms, cord trailing.

"Excuse me," I said, deciding to take the law into my own hands, "but I think you should put that back."

"I dig it, brother," he said in a perfectly friendly way. He turned around and I followed him back into the office he had just left. Inside, four secretaries were having a Diet Pepsi break. One, a girl with false eyelashes and an elaborate hairdo piled to a height of six inches on top of her head, was chewing and popping a wad of gum.

"What," she said, to the man with the typewriter—and popped her gum—"is that?"

I said, "It's one of those new computerized machines where you just speak into it and it types by itself." I thought the concept might interest her, but she made a disgusted face as if it was just not part of her job to think about such things.

"Put it down over *there*," she said, pointing to a table at the rear of the office.

The young man put it down and began to walk out toward the elevators. I still didn't know for sure that he had done anything wrong. Maybe I had just interrupted the typewriter repairman on his appointed rounds. Besides, I had just finished reading a book that claimed jails only made worse criminals out of people and I believed it. I returned to the Box 100 office and the young man went down in the elevator.

"Look at this," said McCann, handing me a letter. "Cooper wants me to make an investigation."

Im just a grocer cashed 2 checks for 2 welfares. Now the bank says the checks were stolen and forged but I know they're not forged I know these women they come in here before. But the bank says there taking 223.00 out of my account to cover the checks I can go to court if I don't like it. Im getting cheeted by the welfare. do i have to get a gun? Joseph DePasquale, 36 Livonia Avenue, Brooklyn.

"Whadda ya think of *that?*" said McCann.

"It's a regular welfare crime wave," I said.

two

ON THE SUBWAY to the Brownsville section of Brooklyn I read the letter about the welfare checks again:

A woman in this bilding name Jones pretend to lose her Welfare Check and they give her another one and then she cash both Checks She have a Boy Frend live with her. I am Ophelia Harm, 119 Herzl Street, Brooklyn.

Ophelia Harm's address was several blocks from the subway station. It was true what they said about Brownsville; it did look bombed-out. I passed one square block that was completely covered with litter and rubble. A fence surrounded the block but one section had fallen down. An old black woman stood just inside the fence sifting through the debris and putting bits and pieces of it into a ramshackle baby carriage. Further into the lot, three young boys were systematically gathering and smashing the beer bottles that were scattered around. A sign had been attached to the fence but now it was hanging by only one bolt:

MODEL CITIES—A Pilot Project in Urban Development—1968.

When I reached the block I wanted, I found, on the right side of Herzl, a row of one-family houses. They were brightly painted and had flower boxes attached to the porch railings, in

11

which dusty plastic flowers were stuck upright in the dirt. At the curb in front of the houses were two wheelless, stripped automobiles, the seats glinting with tiny square crystals of smashed window glass. Cans and papers had been tossed in through the open windows. The trash in one car had been burned; the metal of the cans had turned bluish black from the heat.

On the corner, across the street from the one-family homes, was 113 Herzl, an empty six-story apartment building with all of its front windows smashed out. Next to the building was a garbage-filled lot, and then two more apartment buildings, in which some of the front windows were gaping, others were covered over with sheets of tin and a few still had glass. The buildings looked as though they must be vacant.

The first of the two buildings was 117 Herzl; the second was 119, Ophelia Harm's building. I went inside and looked at the mailboxes in the entry. Most of them were broken. Only two had names on them: "Jones" and "Hamilton." The door to the ground floor front apartment was open. The apartment was vacant. Trash and pieces of shattered furniture were scattered around. An old-fashioned bathtub lay on its side in the middle of the room. Wooden laths were showing through the broken plaster on the walls. Two pieces of wire hung from a hole in the ceiling. The room was filled with the stench of urine.

I went to the ground floor rear apartment and was about to knock on the door when someone made a "Psssst" sound from upstairs. I looked into the shadows on the second floor.

"You from the city?" said a woman's voice.

"Yes."

"Come up."

I went up the stairs. A heavy, muscular black woman was standing in the shadows. She was almost an inch taller than me and I'm five eleven. She wore a black skirt that came to her ankles and a black long-sleeved blouse.

"Box hunderd?" she asked.

"Yes."

"Come in," she said. She led me into her apartment. We went down a long hallway, past a picture of a blue-eyed, blond-haired Jesus in an old-fashioned frame. The hall floor was covered with a linoleum whose pattern was completely worn away except for a few inches near the walls where some green vines and yellow leaves were still faintly visible. The linoleum was waxed and gleaming.

We passed the living room. A faded red velvet cord hanging across the doorway prevented one from entering, as if the room were part of a museum display of rooms from another era—in this case, the 1940s. There was threadbare red-flowered wall-to-wall carpeting on the floor. There was a brown stuffed sofa and two matching stuffed chairs, all extremely old and worn. A small table near the door held a huge old family Bible with gilt-edged pages. On the wall was a picture of the Last Supper. It looked as though the room was entered only when it had to be cleaned; it was spotless. The table with the Bible was gleaming with wax or lemon oil.

The hall led into the kitchen. In the middle of the room was a table covered with oilcloth which, like the linoleum, had its pattern all but worn away. There was an old icebox and an ancient stove. Several huge pots were simmering on top of the stove, and the kitchen was hot and humid. The smell of boiling meat was in the air. By the table was a huge pail of soapy water with a mop in it. The linoleum had just been mopped and was almost dry except for a few spots.

"Sit down," said the woman.

She took the mop out of the pail and wrung it into the sink with her hands. Sweat stood out on her face and her blouse stuck to her back in several places. Putting the mop down, she wiped her hands on a towel and sat down at the table across from me.

"You're Mrs. Harm?" I said.

"Yes." She opened a drawer in the table, took out a scrap of brown paper that had been torn from a paper bag and studied it a moment. "Thursday a week," she said, "I heard that Jones woman talkin' on the stoop. She was tellin' another woman how to cheat Welfare. 'You just cash your check,' she says, 'and you go up to the office and say it didn't come. And if they give you any trouble,' she says, 'you start cryin' and talkin' about your children bein' hungry.'"

I waited to see if there was anything more. Mrs. Harm sensed that I was not overly impressed by her information.

"There it is," she said defensively, and pushed the scrap of brown paper across the table toward me. At the top, "Thursday" was written in pencil. Then "Jones" and "check lost."

"They ought to be locked up," said Mrs. Harm. "They make it so folks like us who really need it can't get enough. There's a woman in the next buildin' been tryin' to get it and still can't get it. I been feedin' her myself out of the little bit I get. I asked for a few dollars for linoleum for a year and couldn't get it. Now it's too late. They don't give out no more checks for that. People like them spoiled it."

She got up from the table, angry now at my lack of response. Going to the stove, she took the cover off one of the steaming kettles and jabbed a long, two-pronged fork into the hot water. She drew out a huge pig's foot, turned it over and put it back down into the boiling water.

"Seems like the city don't care," she said. "They don't do nothin' about it. Give welfare to foreigners, Spanish people who don't even speak English."

"Mrs. Harm," I said, "you can't put someone in jail just because she talks about ways you could cheat the city."

"Talk about it!" she shouted. "She *done* it. Tuesday a week she went and cashed her check, two blocks down, and then went to the Welfare and got another one. She don't care who knows about it. She's *proud* of it. She *said* she done it. . . . The city don't care," she repeated, more coyly now because she saw I was beginning to pay attention.

14

"You have Mrs. Jones' first name?" I asked.

"They call her 'Boo' or 'Pooh' or some nonsense like that."

"All right, Mrs. Harm. I'll look into this."

"And she have a boyfriend."

"We'll look into it."

"They call him Bumpy."

I left Mrs. Harm's apartment and went down the stairs. As I went along the first floor hallway toward the front door, a black man on crutches entered. His right leg was gone from the knee down. The pants leg was pinned up with a safety pin. He wore an old World War II khaki army tunic with sergeant's stripes. It was open down the front. Underneath he wore a filthy T-shirt. Around his neck hung a clenched black fist carved from ebony. He carried a bottle of wine in a paper bag.

"Hey, brother," he said.

"Hello," I said. "Warm day."

"Take a mouthful of this," he said, sticking out the bottle. "It'll give you some cool thoughts."

I took a swallow. It was a lovely sweet rosé. I'd tasted worse at five dollars a bottle.

"That's good," I said.

"You ain't lyin'."

"Does it have sugar added?" I asked.

"Hey," he said reproachfully. "I don't drink no rotgut, brother. I'm not that far gone."

"What kind is it?" I asked.

"Gold Seal . . . Catawba Pink. Most likely they don't have it in your neighborhood."

"What makes you say that?"

"Check it out, brother."

"Veteran?" I asked, changing the subject.

"ETO," he said. "European Theater of Operations. The only nigger at the Bulge."

"The Battle of the Bulge?" I said.

"That's the one, bro. I integrated the Battle of the Bulge."

"Lose your leg there?"

"Right. Kid from Georgia got me from behind. Robert E. Lee Jones. I was supposed to get the Purple Heart but they made up a new rule at the last minute—you had to be wounded by the Germans. They didn't want no nigger war heroes."

The door to the ground floor rear apartment creaked open and a woman called out in a loud whisper that seemed filled with fear. "Bumpy?"

"I'm comin', baby," said the man. "That's my old lady," he explained to me. "Her nerves are bad." Swinging between the crutches, he moved down the hall into the shadows.

three

THE CITY OF NEW YORK is broken down into forty welfare districts. Each district has its own welfare center. Ophelia Harm and Mrs. Jones lived in the district covered by the Bedford welfare center, one of those inexpensive, anonymous contemporary office buildings made of glass and cheap aluminum alloy. An American flag and an orange, white and blue New York City flag slanted out over the sidewalk. There was a long line of people waiting to get into the center: a very old woman with a baby in her arms and three shopping bags at her feet that were overflowing with clothes and household effects, including an empty ketchup bottle which had poked a hole in the bottom of one of the bags; a pretty young woman in her twenties with five children beside her—all girls, with pink bows in their hair; an older woman, swaying from the influence of drugs or alcohol, with several purple bruises on her face and one eye swollen entirely shut; two red-eyed men in dirty clothes sharing a pint bottle of wine. One said to the other, "I've been married thirty years and never had an argument."

I paused to see if I could learn his secret. I had stayed married only ten years, with many an argument.

"Yes, sir," said the man. "I married her ass and left her the same day."

I went into the building and took an elevator up to the second floor, where the office of the director was supposed to be. When I got off the elevator I faced an area the size of a basketball court, with row after row of gray steel desks. Only about half the desks were occupied. In each of the four corners of the room, bolted to the wall about ten feet up, was a television set. The sets were turned on to a Welfare Department training program being broadcast over the city's television channel. On the screen was Max Nixon, the welfare commissioner, sitting behind a desk.

A few people in each of the four corners had drawn up chairs so they could see the program. The others remained at their desks working, reading the paper, drinking coffee and talking to one another, unable to hear the program and apparently not caring. There was a constant ringing of telephones. Some were answered, some kept ringing and ringing.

"What I'm saying is this," said the commissioner, who spoke with a noticeable lisp. "After an initial period of adjustment, I believe the new system will be capable of delivering, consistently, more service to the clients at a lower basic unit cost to the city."

"*Bull*shit," said a tall, thin elderly woman. "I've been here fifteen years and I haven't seen a change yet that made any difference—except for ten new forms to fill out and more work for us."

I went over to a door marked "Archie Hammerman, Director," and knocked. No answer. I knocked a little harder. Still no answer.

"You have to kick the door," said a young man at a nearby desk. "He's deaf."

I pounded on the door with my fist. Again no response. As I stood there wondering what to do next, the door opened, and a very gentle-looking man with gold-rimmed glasses looked out. He wore a dark-gray suit and a white sport shirt without a tie. The open collar of the shirt was folded back over the collar of his suit jacket in the style of 1950 grammar school boys.

"You knocked," he said quietly. It was a statement rather than a question. "Come in, young man," he said. He was only five or six years older than me at the most. He took my arm and drew me into his office. On the wall behind his desk were three glossy colored photographs of porcelain figurines from literature: Hans Brinker and the silver skates, the boy with his finger in the dike and Heidi milking a goat.

"Are you one of our new workers?" said Hammerman.

"No. My name is Ross Franklin. I'm from the City Department of Investigation."

"You should come to work for us. You look like a very nice person. But you've come to investigate us instead. I hope you're going to investigate the good things we do to help people. We do so much."

"I'm sure you do," I said, "but right now I'm interested in something else. I'd like to look at the records of the people on welfare at 117 and 119 Herzl."

I didn't want people to know I was only interested in Mrs. Jones' case because I half expected Mrs. Harm's information to be wrong.

"The new system will be infinitely better," said Hammerman without responding to my request. "Did you hear our commissioner? He's a very intelligent man. He is introducing more computers. Love is not enough, you know. Bettelheim pointed that out very convincingly, don't you think?"

"I'm not familiar with Bettelheim," I said.

"It's a pity. Everything today is so specialized. People don't read anymore."

"Mr. Hammerman, I wonder if I could look at those records."

"You *see!*" said Hammerman as if I'd just proved a point he was trying to make. "Even you, with all your sophistication, still believe that you can find concepts in records. What are records? Words . . . words . . . words. Are you familiar with the work of Ellul?"

"No."

"In a very thought-provoking book he maintains that all of the information put out by a modern democratic society serves only to confuse rather than enlighten."

A handsome, big-bosomed, gray-haired woman in her mid-forties came to the door. "Do you need me, Mr. Hammerman?" she asked.

"Come in, Mrs. Smonk. I want you to meet a friend of mine. Mrs. Smonk is my assistant," he said to me. "A very lovely person. Mrs. Smonk, this is . . . I'm sorry, but I didn't catch your name."

"Ross Franklin, City Department of Investigation."

"Ah, you see?" he said sadly to Mrs. Smonk. "He gives his job as part of his name."

My face reddened a little in annoyance. I had been trying to remind him that I was there on business. He took my arm and squeezed it. "Don't be offended. Everyone does it today. It is part of the universal neurosis of our time. *People and Personnel.* A very brilliant book by Percival Goodman."

"Look," I said, trying to hide my increasing exasperation, "I have to read some records and it may take me quite a while."

"Of course you do, of course you do," said Hammerman gently and reassuringly. "You're in a hurry. I know. Everyone is today. You can sense it in the very air we breathe." He raised his head and breathed in deeply as if to test the air. "It's the peculiar time sense of modern Western man, and part of his dilemma. Even in the East today—"

I'm sure my face flushed in anger, and I was about to utter a profane oath, but Mrs. Smonk must have sensed my feeling. I felt her hand on my arm, and she said, "Mr. Hammerman, I'll just take him out now and get him those records, okay?"

Resignedly, with a gesture of his arm, he surrendered me to Mrs. Smonk. "Read between the lines, Mr. Ross," he said, calling me by my first name instead of my last.

Mrs. Smonk closed the door behind her as she left.

"Thanks," I said, and smiled.

"For what?" she said, without smiling.

"For wearing that blue dress," I said. "It's my favorite color."

Near us, a worker talking on the telephone began to shout, "I said get your ass down here to the center, Mrs. Campbell." He slammed the receiver down.

"What cases do you need?" said Mrs. Smonk.

"The ones at 117 and 119 Herzl."

"Terrible buildings. I've heard about them. Mr. Smedlo handles that area. You'll find him to be an absolutely unmitigated little bastard."

"Where do I find him? Maybe I'll discover his saving grace."

"The only saving grace that could redeem him would be an irresistible suicidal tendency and that hasn't manifested itself yet. Come on; he's upstairs."

I followed her up the stairs. "How did a good-looking woman like you get a name like Smonk?" I said as we went up the stairs.

"How did a good-looking man like you get such a stale line?"

"I'm a terribly unoriginal man—affectionate and sincere as hell, but not original. The first thing that usually pops into my mind is a cliché like 'Why don't we have lunch together?' "

"I'm full of clichés too," she said, "like 'I don't eat lunch, I'm on a diet.' "

We reached the third floor and Mrs. Smonk walked in the direction of a muscular young man in his thirties. "That's Smedlo," she said.

The man's sleeves were rolled up, revealing powerful biceps. He looked like a weight lifter. His eyes were pale gray and utterly cold. There was no flicker of light or emotion in them. They were alert but detached. His face remained absolutely expressionless as Mrs. Smonk said, "This is Mr. Franklin from the City Department of Investigation. This is Mr. Smedlo."

"Hello," I said. He just nodded.

"He needs to look at the cases from 117 and 119 Herzl," said Mrs. Smonk.

21

"Tell the clerk," said Smedlo, and turned back to the papers on his desk.

We went over to a motherly-looking woman who had orange hair with brown roots.

"Mrs. Cohn," said Mrs. Smonk, "this is Mr. Franklin from the City Department of Investigation. He needs all the cases from 117 and 119 Herzl."

"Investigation? Good," said Mrs. Cohn. "A lot of these people could use investigation, and Herzl Street is a good place to start. Look into Rayford Porter's case. He's been on welfare three years because of a sprained ankle. Third generation. I mean, paternalism can go only so far, am I right? There's two kinds of love, the monkey's kind and the eagle's kind. The eagle pushes the little birds out of the nest so they learn to fly. The monkey hugs her babies so tight she strangles them."

"If I had to make a choice, Mrs. Cohn," I said, "I think I'd take monkey love. Being hugged to death seems like a nice way to go."

Beyond Mrs. Cohn, a tall, heavy-set young black woman with her hair wrapped African style in a piece of green-and-yellow silk chuckled silently at my remark. There was something so alive about her dark eyes that I wanted to meet them with my own and share her amusement. She knew I was looking at her, but she refused to look up, which made her all the more intriguing. She moved away from us and sat down at the desk next to Smedlo's.

"Who is that?" I said to Mrs. Smonk.

"That's Valjean Wilcox. She's a case aide."

A timid-looking little man with a tiny mustache—the hairs grew out only in the half-inch area directly beneath his nostrils —came up to us.

"What's wrong?" he asked in a high-pitched, anxious voice.

"Nothing," I said.

"This is Mr. Chitty," said Mrs. Smonk, "Mr. Smedlo's supervisor."

22

"What's the problem?" said Chitty.

Smedlo came up to us and said, "Mrs. Harm's been complaining about her neighbors again, right, Franklin?" I thought I saw a tiny glint of amusement in his cold gray eyes.

"What?" I said, pretending I didn't understand what he was talking about.

Chitty turned on Smedlo. "I told you to close that Jones case!" he screamed in a panicky voice. "I *told* you! How many times do I have to *tell* you?"

Smedlo took a step toward Chitty and there seemed to be so much suppressed violence within him that for an instant I thought he would strike him. Instead he looked down at Chitty and said very calmly and quietly, almost whispering, so you couldn't hear more than a few feet away: "Why don't you shut the fuck up, Chitty? There's no reason to close that case."

Chitty winced and backed away from Smedlo as if he sensed that he was only a hair's breadth away from being slapped. His tone of voice changed. In a pleading, beseeching voice he said, "What about that wino she lives with, Roy?"

"I told you already he doesn't live with her," said Smedlo.

"Well," said Chitty primly, "I'm going to place the whole problem in Mr. Longley's lap. Let him worry about it for a while. He gets paid to. I don't."

Chitty turned toward me as if expecting approval. I managed a weak smile.

"I hope I haven't caused you any inconvenience," I said. "This is a strictly routine investigation I'm making."

"And if I can be of *any* assistance, Mr. Franklin," said Chitty, "just call on me." He stuck out his hand to be shaken. When I stuck out mine he gripped it hard and pumped it repeatedly. He seemed to be trying to convey straightforwardness and sincerity with the grip; I could see he was concentrating and putting his whole arm and shoulder into it. He held his arm stiff without bending it at the elbow.

I glanced for a second over Chitty's shoulder and saw Valjean

Wilcox giving him one of the most intense looks of hatred I had ever seen. I sensed she was a woman who liked to keep her feelings to herself, but her hatred for Chitty was so great that she either did not care to conceal it from me or was unable to. After a moment she looked away. Mrs. Smonk touched my arm.

"You can use that office over there," she said. "Mrs. Cohn put the cases in there for you."

I went into the office and closed the door behind me. Picking a case at random from the pile, I skimmed through it to get an idea of how they were organized. Correspondence and documents were fastened to one side of the folder. The caseworker's descriptions of his visits were typed up on white sheets which were fastened together like a booklet. The visits seemed to follow the same format: an examination of rent receipts and utility bills, presumably to be sure the person wasn't spending rent money on whiskey; questions on the whereabouts of relatives who might be in a position to give money; a series of questions on assets: "We asked the client if she owned any stocks, bonds, real estate, jewels or other valuables, bank accounts or other savings. She denied having any of these things."

The questions on assets amounted to a sort of ritual, since most of the people couldn't be expected to have jewels or real estate. The woman in this case, for example, was a forty-five-year-old retarded woman who had given up a job as a domestic in order to take care of her daughter's baby after her daughter was stabbed to death in a street-corner argument. Even so, Smedlo repeated the questions about stocks and jewels every time he visited.

I flipped through some more cases. Welfare jargon was repeated again and again. "We asked for an explanation of past maintenance." "She denied knowledge of the p.f.'s whereabouts." The p.f. was the "putative father" of a child on welfare. There was bureaucratic brutality lying beneath the surface in all of Smedlo's entries. In one case Smedlo had neglected for half a month to send a check to a woman and her four children.

24

When he discovered his mistake, he grilled the woman to discover how she had survived for fifteen days without any money. Her survival was taken as proof of her guilt—since she hadn't starved to death, she must have some money or a boyfriend. In her record, Smedlo had written:

She claimed she did not know the address or name of the grocer who allegedly let her buy food on credit for two weeks. When we pointed out the contradiction of this, she became abusive. We are suspending this case until Mrs. Rivera provides a more satisfactory story.

I wondered if Smedlo knew the name and address of his grocer. One case in the pile had been handled by Valjean Wilcox. The entries were altogether different in tone. Wilcox wasn't constantly checking to see if the family had concealed jewels or stocks. She kept trying to get Chitty to approve something extra for the family.

"Special approval requested from the Supervisor to pay the fee for an IBM programmer course for Mrs. Smith as this will eventually enable her to get a good job." In the margin Chitty had written: "Denied, check regulation 62–2."

Again Wilcox had written: "Special approval requested from the Supervisor to get beds out of storage for the twins. The whole family is now sleeping in one bed. In the clients' new apartment the twins will have a room of their own. . . . Kowalski Brothers will move for $120. . . ."

Several of Smedlo's clients had also been moved recently by Kowalski Brothers.

Near the bottom of the pile of cases I found the folder of Willamae Jones, the woman about whom Ophelia Harm had complained. The case record showed that she had come to the welfare center on the day Mrs. Harm said and had reported that she did not receive her check. She was given another one for the same amount, $242.70.

I pulled Mrs. Harm's case out of the pile. It was filled with letters complaining about everything: Fannie Lou Brown's son

25

urinates on the fire escape; Willamae Jones' daughter cursed her; Willamae Jones' boyfriend sits on the front stoop and drinks wine and she can't get past to enter the building; Mr. Smedlo is disrespectful to her on the telephone; the woman next door bangs on the wall; the woman upstairs lets the water in the bathtub overflow; the postman puts her mail in other people's boxes.

I flipped through the history part of Mrs. Harm's record. "Report from hospital indicates high blood pressure, diabetes and arthritis . . . client denies any knowledge of husband's current whereabouts . . . claims he was 'no good' and she threw him out twenty years ago . . . client refuses to consider looking for a job . . . client wants to move . . . Kowalski Brothers will move for $100 . . . client decided not to move . . . check for $90 authorized for new linoleum for four rooms and hallway . . . worker will deliver check to client personally."

The last entry was strange, since Mrs. Harm had complained about never receiving money for linoleum. It also seemed uncharacteristic for Smedlo to take the trouble to deliver a check in person. I made a note of the date of the linoleum check.

The office door opened and Valjean Wilcox looked in.

"Come in," I said.

"I need the Smith case for a minute. Mr. Chitty wants me to make an entry about my last visit."

"Help yourself," I said. "I'm finished with that case. . . . I noticed quite a difference in style between your cases and Smedlo's."

"Is that so?" she said with a touch of sarcasm.

"Yes."

"And which is the approved style this month?"

"You sound a little suspicious, Mrs. Wilcox," I said.

"Why do white people always think they've found out something about you when they find out whether you're 'Miss' or 'Mrs.'?"

I blushed. I didn't know exactly what she meant and I always find a naked discussion of race embarrassing.

"What do you mean?" I said.

"You know what I mean, and if you don't, you're not ready to find out. Yes, I'm a little suspicious. How do you think I survived this long in a country like the one I live in?"

"By your wits, I suppose, the same way I survived in this country."

"You and I live in two different countries, Mr. Franklin. Hadn't you noticed? There are dogs that will growl when I pass but they won't bother you."

"Oh, bullshit!" I said, getting annoyed.

"If you can't dig that, Mr. Franklin, you don't have as much on the ball as I thought."

Now the woman had me thoroughly confused.

"It took more than wits to survive in the streets where I grew up," she said.

"What streets were those?"

"Herzl, Sutter, Amboy, Bedford."

"What did it take?" I asked.

"I doubt you'd understand."

"Try me," I said.

"Later," she said.

"Well, I do prefer your style to Smedlo's."

"And the one with the best style will get a prize from the mayor?" said Wilcox. "Come on, Mr. Franklin. When an investigator from the city comes out investigating, black people know enough to watch out. The Smedlos have a way of getting the prizes."

Wilcox took the case and left. A moment later, Mrs. Smonk came in.

"There's some fine social work in here," I said, tapping one of Smedlo's case records.

"I can imagine," she said.

"This girl applied for welfare two years ago, after her first child was born. She was sixteen at the time. The father of the child was still in school and neither of them wanted to get married. Smedlo turned down the girl's application for welfare because she was living with her grandmother and Smedlo claimed the grandmother could take care of the kid while the girl worked. The grandmother was only ninety-one."

"Good thinking," said Mrs. Smonk.

"So the grandmother claimed she couldn't afford to feed the girl and the baby and she finally threw them out. They went to live with a middle-aged man who was separated from his wife and kids. He got her pregnant and then *he* threw them out. They came back to Smedlo to ask for welfare. He tells her she should go back to live with her grandmother. The girl says her grandmother won't take her back. She threatens to leave her baby in the welfare center if she doesn't get money for food. Smedlo says no. Quote: 'We are not giving any funds since the investigation of her eligibility has not been completed.' She leaves the baby in the welfare center and Smedlo puts the baby into the foundling hospital. Then he rejects her case. Now that she doesn't have a baby to take care of, she can work. She's only into her fifth month of pregnancy with her second child.

"She comes back and applies again. She says she wants her baby back. Quote: 'This is doubtful or she wouldn't have abandoned the child in the first place.' She threatens to kill herself if she doesn't get the child back. Quote: 'This is not a serious suicide threat. Miss Perez is constantly making this threat but never follows through.' By the time the second child was born, the grandmother had died. All the girl had to do was cut herself with a mirror in the intake section of the welfare center and she finally got welfare. Smedlo was against it. He recommended commitment to Bellevue instead but Hammerman said no. He said emotionalism was part of the Latin life style. She's still trying to get her first child back."

"What a bastard," said Mrs. Smonk. "I'll have Hammerman look into it."

"Tell me something," I said. "Suppose a client claims she

28

didn't get her check and they give her another one and then she cashes both. Is there any way to check on that?"

"Of course. At our central office downtown. The Miscellaneous Audit section."

"Listen, tell me one more thing: what is it with Kowalski Brothers? Aren't there any other movers in Brooklyn?"

"They're crooks," said Mrs. Smonk. "The caseworkers aren't supposed to do business with them. They charge a client a hundred and twenty bucks to move and then they give twenty back to the caseworker so he'll use them again."

"No wonder they have so much business. Say, it's almost five o'clock. How about having dinner with me?"

"Busy."

"How about tomorrow night?"

"Also busy."

"How about October 25, 1973?"

She smiled. "I'm sorry. I really am busy. Maybe another time."

"Okay. Thanks for your help."

"Okay."

I went down the side stairway to try to avoid Hammerman. I had almost made it to the back exit when Chitty popped out of a men's room in front of me.

"Hi!" he said.

"Hello," I said.

"That Jones case is in on Mr. Longley's desk now," he said. "He's my supervisor."

"Fabulous," I said.

Chitty smiled happily. "Any other problems?" he asked.

"Look, Mr. Chitty," I said, trying to make my voice sound patient. "I didn't say the Jones case was a problem—and none of the other cases are problems either."

"Great!" said Chitty happily. "A clean bill of health, in other words."

I gave up trying to communicate. "Yes," I said. "Very clean."

He stuck out his hand. Reluctantly I stuck out mine. He gave it his intense, stiff-armed, athletic little shake and started back up the stairs, but before I could move, Hammerman came into the hall, heading for the men's room, his fingers already searching for the zipper to his fly.

"Ah, Mr. Ross-the-Investigator. I hope Mr. Smedlo was helpful. He's a very nice young man."

"A doll," I said.

"Did you get to the heart of things, to the wheel within the wheel? Did you listen with the Third Ear?"

"It was just a routine check, Mr. Hammerman. Two ears were enough. Thanks for your help."

"Today," said Hammerman, "everything has become routine: love, food, politics. You should come to work for us. You have, basically, a very good heart. We need fewer investigators and more spies for God, as Shakespeare said."

" 'When the hurlyburly's done, when the battle's lost and won,' " I told him.

I had succeeded in forgetting the Welfare Department over a seafood mousse and a bottle of wine at an inexpensive little French restaurant. But when I left the restaurant and crossed the street I almost bumped into Smedlo as he came out of a nightclub. On his arm he had a fortyish woman with platinum blond hair and very large breasts. Her pale eyes were as cold as his. I took her to be a call girl.

Another couple was with them. The man, in his thirties, was over six feet tall, burly looking and expensively dressed. He had a big head covered with curly black hair that came down over the back of the velvet collar of his chesterfield-style jacket. His pale hazel eyes were almost yellow, and he wore a pair of metallic-rimmed "granny" glasses. With him was a small woman, no longer young, with brown hair and a good figure.

"Well, well, Mr. Smedlo," I said. The other couple moved down the block.

30

"Junior G-man," said Smedlo without a trace of humor.

"And how are you tonight, Mrs. Smedlo?" I said to the woman.

Her control couldn't match Smedlo's. Her mouth twisted into a snarl. "Fuck off," she said.

four

THE NEXT MORNING I looked up Kowalski Brothers in the Brooklyn phone book. They were at 126 Schermerhorn Street. When I got there I found a run-down six-story office building. The directory inside was grimy. The owners had tried to give a touch of class to the building by assigning all of the offices numbers in the thousands. There was no listing for Kowalski Brothers, but Ace Movers were in room 2002. Metropolitan Movers were also in room 2002. Also National Movers, Olympic Movers, Priority Movers and Reliable Movers.

A mailman entered the lobby and we got into the elevator together.

"Excuse me," I said. "Do you know where I can find Kowalski Brothers movers?"

"All the movers in the building are in room 2002. They got a hundred of 'em."

I smiled.

"You think I'm kidding?" he said. "A hundred companies and one truck. It's always parked in the alley out back."

The mailman and I got off at the second floor. The door of room 2002 was directly across from the elevator. The top half of the door was opaque glass. "Ace Movers" was stenciled on it. The mailman knocked on the door. It was dark inside. He began taking bunches of brown envelopes from his bag and stuffing them into the slot in the bottom half of the door.

"Bank statements," he said. "Today it's Chase Manhattan. Yesterday it was Manufacturers Hanover. Day before that it was Chemical. They do a lot of banking for such a tiny office."

"You must have put fifty envelopes in there," I said.

"That's nothing. You should have seen it day before yesterday. I put in a hundred Chemical Bank statements if I put in one. Before this month they never got so much as a postcard. This month they get a letter from every bank in the city."

"Are you sure Kowalski Brothers are here too?" I asked.

"Sure. Look at this."

He pulled about forty envelopes from his pouch and handed them to me. They were envelopes from First National City Bank. Each one seemed to be from a different branch, in Manhattan, the Bronx, Queens and Staten Island as well as Brooklyn. They were all addressed to Kowalski Brothers. I handed them back to the mailman.

"Thanks," I said.

"You're welcome," he said. "You should hear some of the things I run into. I could write a book. The guy in that next office there offered me a special delivery stamp if I'd go out and bring him a container of coffee."

He nodded toward the door of room 2006. "Creative Enterprises" was lettered on the opaque glass. In smaller letters was "Mutual Funds, Burglar Alarms, Gardening Advice."

"Sounds very creative," I said.

"Never gets any mail," said the mailman. "I hope he don't catch bank fever from the movers."

I thanked him again and left the building.

I headed for the Department of Welfare's main office in downtown Manhattan, not far from the office of Box 100. A semipermanent barricade of steel pipes and plywood had been constructed around the building, apparently to assist the police in controlling demonstrations by employees and people on welfare. Today there was a small, listless group of employees with cardboard signs hanging from their necks walking in a circle on the sidewalk. "Social Work not Paper Work" said one of the signs. Two policemen leaned against the barricade and discussed food prices in Nassau County.

"You can get three cans of Bumble Bee tuna for a dollar at Pathmark," said one.

"No kidding," said the other.

I went up to one of the women who was marching in front of the building. "Is it okay to go in?"

"Why not?" she said. Evidently it was not really a picket line.

The section I wanted was on the ninth floor. Every welfare check in the city, after it was cashed, was sent for storage to the Miscellaneous Audit section so that if there was any question as to who cashed it, the check itself could be examined.

I approached the receptionist. "Is this where the canceled checks are returned?"

"Where are you from?" she asked.

"City Department of Investigation."

"I couldn't give out that information."

"You can't tell me if this is where the canceled checks are returned?" I said.

"Maybe Mr. Gross can help you," she said. She picked up the phone and buzzed a buzzer. "Mr. Gross, there's a man here from some company and he wants to return some canceled checks."

She listened to Mr. Gross for a moment, then said to him, "How should I know where he got them?" She turned back to me. "Where did you get them?" she asked.

"Darling," I said, "I'm from the City Department of Investigation, the New *York* City Department of Investigation. I'm investigating a case. I need to *look* at some of *your* canceled checks."

She turned back to the telephone. "He's investigating cases

or something," she said to Gross. She listened a moment. *"I don't know, Mr. Gross. Why don't you talk to him yourself?"*

A moment later, an office door opened and out came Gross, a dapper little man in a pink shirt and red polka dot tie.

"We don't have any cases here," he said with a puzzled look on his face.

"My name is Franklin," I said. "I'm an investigator with the New York City Department of Investigation. I need to look at some of your canceled welfare checks."

"I'm not authorized to give that out, Mr. Lynn," he said.

"Franklin," I said. "Ross Franklin."

"What?" he said.

"My name is Ross Franklin," I said.

"It is?" he said. "Do I know you?"

"No. Listen, can I speak to someone who would be authorized to let me see some checks?"

"I'm just trying to think who that would be," said Gross.

"How about Mrs. Daniels?" said the secretary.

"No," said Gross. "She's with foster home payments."

"Isn't that what he wants?" said the secretary.

At that moment a balding, sour-looking man with a tiny lipless mouth came in the door. Under his arm he had a *New York Times* folded to the crossword puzzle, which was half finished. The top of his head was completely bald, but he let the hair on one side grow very long and then combed the strands up over the bald part and plastered them down with Vaseline.

"Oh," said Gross, "this is Mr. Dombrow, the director of our division." It wasn't exactly an introduction, since Mr. Gross seemed uncertain if Dombrow would want to handle anything this small.

"What does he want?" said Dombrow to Gross, ignoring me.

"I'm an investigator with the city," I said, trying to make it sound strong. "Department of Investigation. Possible fraud." I was getting tired of standing around.

"All right," he said. "Come in."

He led the way to his office. He sat down at his desk, on which there was a paperweight but no papers, and put the *Times* in the middle desk drawer.

"I'm investigating a complaint to the Department of Investigation," I said, "and I need to look at a few canceled welfare checks."

"Anything else?" said Dombrow. He was very businesslike and wanted to get it all out on the table before he responded.

"Well," I said, "I'd be interested in knowing how you handle a situation where someone reports she lost her check, gets a replacement and then cashes both checks."

"It's not a problem," said Dombrow. I expected him to go on, but he didn't.

"I don't understand," I said.

"We send out almost half a million checks every two weeks," he said. "Suppose five hundred are reported stolen—it's more than that, but let's just say five hundred. We compare the signature on the stolen check with the client's signature. If the signatures don't match, we report it to the bank as a forgery. Ninety-nine times out of a hundred, the bank got the check from a neighborhood merchant. They tell him it's a forgery and subtract the amount from his balance. If he doesn't like it, he can go to court."

"You mean the neighborhood merchant is the one that gets stuck," I said.

"Nobody gets stuck, Mr. Franklin," he said in a nasty, impatient tone. "No one's making the neighborhood grocer cash these checks. He does it to get people into his store. The problem corrects itself. Once these merchants get burned a few times, they'll stop cashing dubious checks.

"Out of five hundred lost checks we may find fifty where the signature on the check is exactly like the client's signature. She cashed it out of plain stupidity. If she were really trying to cheat us, she'd take the trouble to disguise her handwriting a little—and then it would look like a forgery and we wouldn't have to pay off the bank."

36

"How many checks get reported stolen?" I asked.

"Well, let's see. Right now we're working on the February checks—we're five months behind."

He noticed my surprised expression.

"Don't worry," he said. "The commissioner knows about the backlog. I wouldn't sit on a problem like that. The PYA principle—protect your ass. I wouldn't be where I am now if I hadn't learned to do that. Every month I send him a memo and ask for more clerical help to clean up the backlog of checks—I kick the problem upstairs. Let him worry about it. That's what he gets paid for."

Dombrow opened a drawer and took out a sheet of paper.

"One thousand one hundred and fifty-five checks were stolen in February," he said.

"You mean if a client lied about not getting a check back in February, you'd only be finding out about it now, five months later?"

"It doesn't make any difference," said Dombrow. "She'll still be there. Where's she gonna go in five months—Miami? When we find out about it, we take twenty dollars out of her check every two weeks until we get our money back."

"And the merchant who cashed a bad check five months ago only finds out this month that the bank is going to subtract two hundred dollars from his balance?"

"Mr. Franklin," said Dombrow, "you can be very boring. The merchant has his problems, I have mine. Is he worried about my problems? No. Now if that's all you need, I'll get back to work."

"I would like to know the number of clients who said they didn't get their checks from March up until the present."

Dombrow picked up the phone. "Tell Nolan to get in here," he said to his secretary.

A moment later, a short, fat man in his thirties entered. He wore glasses that were so thick, they magnified his brown eyes to double their actual size. He looked like an owl. His unsmiling expression accentuated the similarity. His head was covered with a three-inch-thick mass of blond curls.

"He wants to look at some canceled checks," said Dombrow. "And give him the figures on stolen checks since February."

"Thank you," I said to Dombrow. He didn't reply. As I followed Nolan out of the office and closed the door behind me, I saw Dombrow open his middle drawer and take out the *New York Times.*

Nolan led me to an area containing rows and rows of filing cabinets with little drawers just big enough to hold canceled welfare checks.

"What are the names and dates of the checks you need?" he asked.

I gave him the information and he found the check Willamae Jones had reported stolen and the check Smedlo had claimed he took to Ophelia Harm for linoleum.

"How can I tell if this is really Willamae Jones' signature?" I asked Nolan.

He took me over to another file cabinet. "Before we give her a replacement, she has to sign this form where she swears she did not get the check." He pulled out the form Willamae Jones had signed and looked at the signature. "The two signatures don't look alike," said Nolan.

"No," I said. "They don't."

Underneath the signature on the check was the signature of Nathan Sapperstain, and then the words "Sapperstain's Market, 695 Saratoga Avenue" were rubber-stamped.

"Sapperstain cashed it for her," said Nolan. He looked at the back of Mrs. Harm's linoleum check. Underneath the endorsement was the stamp of a Chemical Bank branch.

"She's got a bank account," said Nolan. A number had also been written on the back of the check. "That's her account number," he said. He turned the checks over. "Bedford welfare center. Who's the caseworker?"

"Roy Smedlo," I said.

I thought Nolan gave me a funny look, but I couldn't be sure behind those owlish glasses.

"Know him?" I said.

"No."

Before I left, Nolan gave me the figures for lost or stolen checks from March through July. The number had jumped from 1,280 on March 1 to 3,331 on July 1. It meant that the number of merchants who were going to be upset by their losses on bad checks had more than doubled in a few months.

five

NEXT I WENT to the grocery store where Willamae Jones' check had been cashed and talked to Mr. Sapperstain, a fat sour-looking man with a big belly. There was stubble in the folds of his double chins where he had been too lazy to shave.

"This check was cashed here on July first," I said. "Do you remember the person that cashed it?"

He scrutinized the check.

"Sure. Willie Mae Jones."

"Do you mean Willamae Jones?" I said.

His eyes narrowed and he looked at me a little more carefully. He began to realize it might cost him money to be wrong.

"That's what I said, didn't I?" he asked.

"What did the person look like?" I asked. He hesitated a moment, and I realized he didn't remember.

"Medium looking," he said finally. "Average."

"The signature does not look like Willamae Jones' handwriting."

"Look, mister, are you trying to say I cashed a bad check?"

"What I'm trying to say is that the signature on this check does not look like Willamae Jones' handwriting."

"Half these people don't even know how to write," said Sapperstain. "They don't write their name the same way twice. They don't know how."

"And she's medium looking?" I said.

"That's right."

"Any distinguishing marks?"

"No."

"Light or dark skinned?" I asked.

"I'm not prejudiced," said Sapperstain. "I don't notice things like that."

"Okay, thank you," I said.

"I'm too goodhearted," he said.

"Yeah," I said.

I walked from the grocery store down to Herzl Street. As I was passing the abandoned building on the corner I saw Mrs. Harm coming down the front steps carrying a heavy iron pot.

"Hello, Mrs. Harm," I said. "What are you doing up there?"

"Takin' Mrs. Procacino some soup. Look like Mr. Smedlo never be openin' her case."

"You mean somebody lives in there?"

"Mrs. Procacino and Bumpy—and sometimes the baby stay there."

"I think you lost me, Mrs. Harm. Who's Mrs. Procacino?"

"She's an old woman, a little funny in the head. She's afraid to leave. Lived in the buildin' all her life. She's afraid they're gonna put her away. She managed okay with her son there to help her but he had to go to the hospital to have a kidney removed. So now she don't have anyone to look out for her."

"Why doesn't she move out?"

"She don't have any money to get a place. She only get about fifty dollars from Social Security. And she's afraid. She's used to that place."

"And Bumpy lives in there?" I asked.

"When he's not with that Jones woman."

"And you said there's a baby there?"

"Sometimes. He's there now. They snuck him out of Jones' apartment this mornin' after the supervisor came out investigatin'."

"The supervisor came out investigating?"

"Didn't you send him?" said Mrs. Harm.

"No," I said. "What did he look like?"

"A nervous-lookin' little white fella. They said he was Smedlo's supervisor."

"Why did they sneak the baby out?"

"They said he wasn't supposed to be there, or somethin'."

"Whose baby is he?"

"Some say it's Bumpy's baby, but he don't look like Bumpy to me."

"Who's the mother?" I said.

"The Jones woman supposed to be the mother, but there's somethin' funny about that too."

"Can I go inside?"

"Come on," said Mrs. Harm. "Maybe you can get Smedlo to give a little welfare to Mrs. Procacino."

"Smedlo knows about all this?"

"Sure."

We went up the front steps and Mrs. Harm lifted the sheet of tin that had been nailed over the front door. The nails had been pulled out on the bottom and the right side. We had to stoop over to get in. In the hallway inside you could just barely see. There were broken plaster and trash on the floor and on the stairway as we climbed to the second floor.

Mrs. Harm banged on the door to the rear apartment.

"It's me, mama," she called out, and pushed the door open.

Inside was a wrinkled old woman in an old one-armed rocking chair. Her receding hair was thin and unkempt. She had a jutting chin with strands of long black hair growing out of it. She wore a faded old black dress with lace trim that was now ragged and falling off in spots.

She rocked slowly and in her arms she held a sleeping child wrapped in a brand-new bright-yellow baby blanket.

The woman smiled to see Mrs. Harm and said something that sounded like "Nasa, nasa." She seemed to have only three teeth in her mouth.

42

"She don't speak good English," said Mrs. Harm.

"Nasa, nasa," repeated Mrs. Procacino. With a grin she held the child up slightly for me to look at. The child opened his eyes for a moment—they were a beautiful gray—and then went back to sleep. He had a great deal of straight black hair and skin the color of light coffee. He was about two years old.

"Tito, Tito," said the old woman.

"That's what they call him," said Mrs. Harm.

The room we were in was the kitchen. There was an old refrigerator, sink and stove and several orange crates with dishes and canned goods in them. On one of the orange crates was a hot plate. An extension cord ran from the hot plate across the floor and out one of the room's two windows. All the windowpanes were missing. The windows looked out onto a trash-strewn back yard.

For the baby, there were a brand-new playpen, potty chair, crib and teddy bear.

"Where did all these baby things come from?" I asked.

"Valjean got them for the baby," said Mrs. Harm.

"Valjean? Valjean who?"

"I don't know her last name," said Mrs. Harm. "She's the one always be over at the Jones'. Supposed to be some kind of social worker, but she don't look like no social worker to me—wears her hair all wrapped up and stickin' out behind like an African woman."

"Peesa booda," said Mrs. Procacino.

"She want you to have somethin' to eat," said Mrs. Harm. On an orange crate near Mrs. Procacino's chair was a soup bowl with four meat balls in it.

"No, thank you," I said to Mrs. Procacino.

She nodded her head, urging me to take one.

"Peesa booda," she repeated.

"No, really," I said. "I should be going. Thanks anyway. *Grazie.*"

"*Sì, grazie,*" said Mrs. Procacino, recognizing an attempt to communicate in Italian. She grinned and showed her three yellow rotting teeth.

"I'll be back later, mama," said Mrs. Harm.

"*Giorno,*" said Mrs. Procacino.

"Good-bye," I said, and Mrs. Procacino nodded."Where does Bumpy live?" I asked Mrs. Harm.

"On the next floor, but we can't go up there. He gets mad if anyone comes near his apartment."

We went down to the street.

"By the way, Mrs. Harm, what ever happened to your check for linoleum?"

"I never got no check for linoleum. You saw yourself I don't have any. I asked Smedlo for linoleum money for a year and he wouldn't give it. You'd think it was comin' out of his pocket." She was silent for a moment. She seemed to be thinking. Then her eyes narrowed and she turned back to me with an angry expression on her face. "Did he say he gave me money for linoleum?"

"Not exactly," I said. It sounded very unconvincing.

"That man gonna get his reward and he's gonna get it sooner than he thinks. You can't play that way with people but only so long."

Mrs. Harm walked up to her building, and after she had had a chance to get upstairs I went in too and knocked on Willamae Jones' door. There was no answer. Inside I could hear the loud blaring of a television set. I knocked harder. There was still no answer. Instead I heard a woman's voice. "I told ya fifty times to put that down." Then I heard the sound of someone being hit, and a child crying. I hammered on the door.

"Who?" said a voice that sounded frightened. It sounded like the voice of the woman who had called to Bumpy the day before.

"Ross Franklin," I said.

"*Who?*"

"Ross Franklin."

44

I heard a bolt slide, then the door opened. A huge black woman about forty-five years old stood in the doorway. She wore a faded red house dress that was a size too small for her, and the top button had popped off so that part of her faded bra and large bosom were showing. On her right breast just above the edge of the bra was a jagged scar. She had three small scars on her face—one above the lip, one above the right eyebrow and a U-shaped scar on the left cheek. Her eyes were filled with what appeared to be a permanent panic. She seemed to summon up all of her control in order to speak to me.

"Yes?" Her pretense of calmness was betrayed both by the terror that remained in her eyes and by a twitch of the right cheek and eye. Clinging to her leg was a crying child, apparently the one who had been hit just before the door opened. He was a little boy about four years old, naked except for faded red socks. His hair stood out about four inches all over his head in one of the best Afros I had ever seen.

"Are you Mrs. Jones?" I asked.

"Yes."

"My name is Ross Franklin. I'm from the City Department of Investigation."

The twitch hit her face again. She turned to the crying child as if grateful to have some distraction.

"Okay, Booba," she said, and pulled him up onto her bosom. Holding him with one arm, she reached into her dress pocket and pulled out two broken pieces of graham cracker and three raisins. The child took them eagerly and put the raisins and one piece of cracker into his mouth. His delight at having the raisins and being back in his mother's good graces was so enormous that he grinned at me.

"Hi!" he said. His happy expression contrasted oddly with his mother's panic.

"Hi!" I said.

"You wanna sit down?" said Mrs. Jones.

"Thank you," I said, and sat down on the couch.

I looked carefully at Mrs. Jones. It was difficult and required a little imagination, but you could still see the pretty, sensitive woman she had been before time, scars, fat, children, Herzl Street and God knows what else had made her what she was now.

In one corner of the living room were three children, an eight-year-old girl and two boys about nine or ten. They were playing with some pots and pans and canned food. An ironing board was open in the middle of the room with an iron on it and a pile of clothes. Other clothes were scattered all over. Hanging from a chair was one freshly pressed little pink dress.

In another corner a television set was blaring. Sitting on a chair, staring at the set and sucking a lollipop was a girl of about eighteen dressed only in a faded green bathrobe that was drawn carelessly around her. She had slim legs and beautiful full breasts. Her face had a sullen expression and she stared at the tube almost as if in a trance. Her eyes seemed shiny but expressionless, almost dead. She hadn't looked up when I entered.

"I'm here about your last check," I said. "The one for July first."

Mrs. Jones didn't say anything, but her face began to twitch again. Instead of looking at me she looked in the direction of the television set.

"You reported that you didn't receive it," I said.

"I *didn't* receive it," she said, her face twitching spasmodically.

"Well," I said, "it was cashed at Sapperstain's grocery and he says he remembers you." He had also said the woman was average looking with no distinguishing marks. No one would describe Mrs. Jones that way.

"Everyone knows he's a liar," said Mrs. Jones. "I never go in there. His prices are too high."

In the corner the three children had begun to squabble. One of the boys pushed the girl and she hit her head on a chair and began to cry. She picked up a pan and menaced the boy.

"Cut that out," shouted Mrs. Jones almost hysterically. The children ignored her. The girl took the pan and pushed it at the boy's chest. He slapped it aside and it fell on the floor, hitting the other boy on the foot. Mrs. Jones jumped up from the couch, grabbed the two boys by their clothing with one hand and slapped the girl's buttocks with the other hand. The girl began to scream. Mrs. Jones released one boy and slapped his buttocks. He began to cry. The third boy began to whimper even before being hit. Then he was slapped, but he controlled his tears and shouted angrily at his mother, "She started it."

Mrs. Jones then turned to the girl watching television and shouted, "Turn that damn thing off!"

With no change in expression, the girl reached over and raised the volume a little. She continued to stare sullenly at the set. Standing in the middle of the room, between the girl and me, Mrs. Jones began to tremble. I got up to leave. Mrs. Jones looked like a woman who needed help, and every instinct told me not to run, but unfortunately I was part of her problem.

The girl at the television set turned toward me.

"Where you say you from? Investigation?"

"City Department of Investigation," I said.

Her bathrobe had now slipped open enough so that I could see the nipple of her left breast.

"You oughta 'vestigate that Smedlo. He a jive dude."

"Shut up, Willette," said Mrs. Jones, beginning to tremble more violently.

Willette continued to stare unemotionally at me. I felt as though she was trying to look inside me. She pulled her bathrobe around herself and then took her right index finger and, through the bathrobe, flicked the nipple of her left breast, pretending to scratch it. I was sure she was trying to stir my feelings, and she was succeeding. In an attempt to prevent her from realizing it, I set my face in what I imagined was a cold, hard expression and walked to the door. I opened it and went outside. When I got to the street I found that my heart was pounding.

six

I WENT BACK to my office. When the elevator door opened on my floor I found the pimply-faced young guard staring into my face from a distance of six inches. I had to step around him to get off the elevator.

"Who you wanna see?" he demanded to know.

"I work here," I said. "Box 100."

"Box 100? What's that?"

"That's where I work."

"Let's see your employee identification card."

"What's this all about anyway?" I said. I didn't have an employee identification card.

"Typewriters," he said. "We been losin' too many."

"Oh," I said. "Well, look, I don't have an employee identification card yet. I just started. But if you'll call Pat McCann, he'll confirm the fact that I work here."

"Oh," he said, breaking into a smile. "You work with Pat?"

"Yes."

"You a private eye too?" he said, obviously impressed.

"I guess you could call me a public eye," I said.

"My name's José," he said, and stuck out his hand.

"Hello, José. My name is Ross Franklin."

"I'll get you coffee on my coffee break," said José.

"Oh, no, thanks, José. You don't have to do that."

"Yeah, I want to. What kind of Danish you like—cheese?"

"No. Thanks anyway, José. See you later."

"I'll bring ya prune," said José.

I walked down to the office. Pat McCann and Laura were there. The secretary had her face hidden behind some papers.

"Did ya crack that case?" said McCann.

"Not quite," I said. "Listen, how can I get an employee identification card?"

"José stopped ya, huh? I've been givin' him some pointers. You won't need a card. I'll get you one of these." He pulled out his wallet and flipped it open. Pinned to the inside was a shiny silver police shield. "Jersey City Police Department," said McCann. "I got a pal over there—retired cop. This was his badge. I got another one at home somewhere."

"I think I'd feel funny carrying that around, Pat."

"It's up to you. How far'd you get on that case?"

I explained that Mrs. Harm apparently had a bank account and that the check reported stolen by Mrs. Jones had been cashed. I showed Pat copies of the check and the form Mrs. Jones had signed saying she didn't get the check.

"The signatures don't match," I said.

"Yeah," said Pat. "It's a left-hand job."

"What?" I said.

"Left hand," he repeated. "When the average person wants to disguise his signature he usually switches to the left hand. He thinks it'll be so different you won't be able to tell. But he always makes the mistake of making the letters the same way. See how she doesn't close her *o*'s? See the little loop on the *s*?"

Pat was right. The peculiarities of Willamae Jones' signature were all carried over to the check endorsement, but in a distorted way that might be explained by a right-handed person signing with his left hand. But you couldn't be sure.

"If the guy will testify it was her who cashed the check, we've got her nailed," said McCann.

"He probably would," I said.

"This welfare check thing is getting to be a mess, you know?" said Pat. "That guy DePasquale I went out to see yesterday morning has really been getting burned. He swears he knows the two clients who cashed their checks but Welfare claims they were stolen checks and the signatures don't match, so Welfare won't pay off the bank, and the bank subtracts it from DePasquale's balance."

"It's true if the signature is a little off the Welfare Department will claim it's a forgery," I said.

"That ain't right," said McCann. "Especially if the grocer remembers the person who cashed it."

"But, Pat," I said, "the grocer is always going to say he remembers the person who cashed it, because he loses money if the Welfare Department doesn't pay off."

"And the client is always gonna claim it wasn't him who cashed it. It's the grocer's word against the client, and I'm with the grocer. He's contributing something to society. What is the welfare client contributing except babies?"

"Well, anyway, Pat, the problem seems to be getting worse. I was down at the main welfare office today and the number of checks clients claimed they lost jumped from twelve hundred in March to thirty-three hundred in July."

"Hey!" said Pat. "This is important. Let's go see Cooper. I'm tryin' to sell him on the idea of a welfare check raid."

"A what?" I asked.

"A welfare check raid. We sit in a car outside DePasquale's store when the checks come on Thursday. If someone cashes a welfare check, DePasquale gives us a signal. The welfare center is only a few blocks away. If the person cashes her check and then heads for the welfare center, we follow her, and if she says she didn't get her check, we bust her on the spot. It was DePasquale's idea. Claims bad checks are gonna drive him out of business."

"So why does he keep cashing welfare checks?"

"The people owe him money. They bought stuff on credit. If he doesn't cash their checks, they won't pay him off. They'll just go somewhere else and shop."

"So why does he sell on credit?" I asked.

"Because the people don't have any money. If he don't give them credit, they can't buy his stuff. So how do you like the idea of a raid, Ross?"

"Pat, I don't like cracking down just on the little guys."

"The little guys!" said Pat. "What little guys? DePasquale's the little guy."

"The guy on welfare is the little guy, Pat. He doesn't have much of anything."

"Are you kidding?" said Pat. "What about the welfare Cadillac? I can't even afford a Volkswagen, for Christ's sake!"

"Pat, do you know bankers steal more money than bank robbers?"

"What are you talking about, bankers steal more money than bank robbers? What kind of a riddle is that? Bankers don't have to steal money. They *got* it."

"Hiya, Pat. Hiya, Ross." José was at the door. "I brung ya some coffee and Fresca and pastry." He had a big bag from Horn & Hardart.

Pat whispered to me, "Pipe down about that banker business, will ya? I don't want the kid to hear ya talking like that. Come in, kid," he said to José.

José turned to me. "I brought a prune and a cheese Danish. You can take your pick."

"This one's on me, José," said McCann, taking out his wallet —the badge flashed as he opened it—and picking out a dollar bill.

"Thanks, José," I said. "And thank you, Pat."

"Chow—as they say," said Pat, and he took a long drink from his can of Fresca. "José," he said, "keep your eye on the *Daily News*. We're planning a big raid within the next week. It could hit the *News* on Friday. I can't say anything about it. Secret stuff."

52

"Gee, thanks for letting me know, Pat. I'll get the early edition on Thursday night."

We finished our coffee and José left.

"Let's go see Cooper," said Pat.

Cooper had on the same blue pants and slightly different blue jacket and the same necktie—without egg this time.

"Ross has that case just about cracked," said McCann. "The woman reported her check was lost and then cashed it using the left-handed signature routine. And the woman who ratted on her has a bank account. That's gotta be against the rules, I don't care how liberal they get. Ross says the number of stolen checks is shooting up. Unless we pull off that welfare check raid, the grocers are gonna get so sore they'll try to take it out on the mayor. But a raid with a couple of good busts and a story in the *Daily News* will put the fear of God into them. We could take a reporter and a photographer with us. The clients'll start thinking twice before they make a phony claim that they lost their check, 'cause they won't know who's looking when they cash it."

"I don't know," said Cooper.

"I'm against it," I said. McCann gave me a disgusted look. "It's small potatoes—a check here, a check there. If the merchant doesn't know the person, he shouldn't cash the check."

"I'll take it up with Vanderbilt," said Cooper. "I'm seeing him this afternoon."

seven

I WAS SITTING at my desk the next morning reading some Box 100 letters when McCann came in.

"Hiya, Ross. We're gonna make that welfare check raid this afternoon. The welfare commissioner likes the idea. He thinks there's been too many phony lost checks. I worked out all the details with DePasquale. Meet me here around two and we'll pick up a couple of detectives and an assistant DA. We get to use a disguised police truck where you can look out through little holes and not be seen. I'll be driving, dressed as a painter. Two blocks from DePasquale's store is the Flatbush welfare center. We can tell from inside the truck if anyone cashes his check at DePasquale's and then heads in that direction."

"Fabulous," I said.

"We checked out the rules on welfare bank accounts too. It's okay if she don't have too much money in the account. If she's got too much, they take it away. It's up to the caseworker."

"How much could the old lady have?" I said.

"Ya know, Ross," said McCann seriously, "for an investigator, you take a very negative approach."

"Five bucks says she doesn't have more than two hundred dollars."

"Two hundred dollars! I don't have that much myself!"

54

I picked up the phone and dialed the Chemical Bank where the linoleum check was deposited.

"This is Ross Franklin of the City Department of Investigation. I'd like to find out the balance for account 059–505324."

There was a pause while the woman checked. McCann picked up the other phone to listen. The woman came back to the phone.

"That's 059–505324?" she said.

"Yes," I said.

"The balance as of yesterday was $15,507."

"Jesus Christ almighty," said McCann.

"Are you *sure?*" I asked.

"Yes," she said. "The account of Roy Smedlo."

"Roy Smedlo," I said.

"Yes; 059–505324. Isn't that what you wanted?"

"Yes," I said. "Thank you."

"You must have given her the wrong number," said McCann.

"Smedlo is her caseworker," I said.

"Why would she put her check in *his* account?" said McCann.

"Good question," I said. I took the canceled check out of my desk and compared the signature with that on Mrs. Harm's letter to Box 100. They were not the same.

I went over to the Bedford welfare center and up to Chitty's unit.

"We suspended that Jones case," he said proudly.

"Why?" I couldn't keep the hostility out of my voice.

My tone surprised and disappointed him. "You don't think it should be closed?" he asked.

"I'd just like to know why you decided to close it," I said.

"Technically we call it 'Whereabouts unknown.' "

"Whereabouts unknown? She's right there. I talked to her yesterday."

"Well, we asked her to come down to the center to answer a few questions and she didn't come. Technically we don't know where she is because we haven't seen her. So we can close her case. For all we know, she might not need welfare anymore."

"Lovely," I said.

Now it was Chitty's turn to get hostile. He launched a prissy little counterattack. "Why don't you mind your own business?" he said. "You come around here being sarcastic and telling everyone how to do their jobs. For your information, she has a *boy*friend, and she's been taking care of someone else's baby and not telling us about it. She may be earning all kinds of money doing that. She won't cooperate with us."

"How about Mrs. Procacino? Do you think she's got a boyfriend too?" I said. "Is that why she doesn't qualify for welfare?"

"You know very well a person can't live in an abandoned building. It's not fit to live in. It's against the law. She's violating the law."

Smedlo came up.

"Gumshoe," he said.

"Smedlo," I said, "did you ever send Mrs. Harm a check for linoleum?" I wanted to see if I could faze him. His eyes betrayed nothing.

"You want me to remember every check I send on seventy cases?" he said. "Come over here; I'll look it up." He was trying to get away from Chitty.

"What's this all about?" said Chitty.

"Get outa here, Chitty," said Smedlo contemptuously. "Go back to your desk and shuffle some forms."

Chitty went away. Smedlo found Ophelia Harm's case, flipped it open, found the entry and said, "Yes, I delivered that check to her myself."

"I saw that entry," I said, "but the check was deposited in your bank account."

Smedlo leaned close to me in that marvelous technique he had for intimidating people. He spoke through clenched teeth.

"Don't push me, Franklin. I don't like it. You don't play in my league. You could get *hurt!*" For emphasis he slammed his fist down on the desk a half inch from where my hand was resting. I was convinced he was capable of actually striking me as I stood there and it made me nervous. He was clearly under pressure now, but instead of loosening up, Smedlo's control seemed to increase, and so did the potential violence just beneath the surface.

"If that check was deposited in my account, it's because I cashed it for that old bag. It wouldn't be the first time."

I thought Smedlo's suppressed violence might explode if I told him the signature on the check wasn't hers. And I didn't see anything to be gained by confronting him directly now. Valjean Wilcox was sitting at her desk nearby and I went over to see her.

"Hello, Mrs. Wilcox," I said, and smiled. I couldn't help liking the woman. Perhaps it was her directness that I appreciated.

"Hello," she said, and she smiled too. "Sit down," she said, and I did.

"I'm trying to decide who gets the award for being nicest welfare worker of the year," I said. "I've narrowed it down to either you or Chitty, and I'm leaning toward Chitty because he's white."

"He is, isn't he?" She grinned.

"How are you doing today?" I said.

"I'm getting tired of all the bullshit."

"So am I."

She opened her purse and pulled out a long silk scarf. Something clattered to the floor. I looked down. It was a pistol.

"Jesus Christ!" I said—too loudly, because Chitty and Smedlo both looked over at us.

Valjean looked at me disgustedly and very calmly dropped her scarf on the floor. It fell on top of the pistol and concealed it.

"When are you gonna learn to be cool?" she said. "If I dropped a reefer you'd probably faint." She bent over and

57

picked up the pistol inside the scarf. I was embarrassed by what she said and I must have blushed. She noticed it and said, almost gently, "You're shy, aren't you? I like that in a man."

Then I really did blush. I've never taken compliments gracefully.

"It's a cap pistol," she said. "I need it in my neighborhood to scare off muggers."

"Yes," I said. "I imagine a cap pistol that shoots twenty-two-caliber bullets *would* scare off most muggers." I know something about guns, and her weapon was no cap pistol. "Listen," I said, changing the subject, "since when do case aides buy baby equipment for their clients?"

"What's that supposed to mean?" said Valjean, trying to be cool, but I noticed that rush of blood to the face which is the black equivalent of a blush. You have to be perceptive to notice the subtle change in color, but attention to small details has always been one of my strong points.

"That innocent act might work on Chitty," I said, "but all us honkies aren't alike, you know."

She smiled. You couldn't keep her down. She shot back with another racial joust. "The idea that the social worker and the client can't get involved with one another is a *white* concept. You people invented it—and you can keep it. The kid needed those things, and it didn't look like your welfare system was going to provide them, so *I* did. The kids on welfare in Browns-ville don't even know there's an ocean fifty blocks away.... My kids are gonna know there's an ocean in this town."

"You have children?" I said.

"No," she said, and mumbled something which sounded to me like "Only abortions."

I looked up and saw tears in her eyes. She turned away from me, walked slowly across the office and into the ladies' room. I went upstairs to see Mrs. Smonk.

"You look a little tired," she said.

"Smedlo's losing his charm for me. Do you have a phone book? I'd like to see where he lives."

She opened a file and pulled out his card.

"One thirty Central Park West, apartment forty-two A," she said.

"That's a luxury rent area," I said.

"So you're investigating Smedlo. Believe me, I wouldn't put anything past him."

"He probably lives in a luxury area because he has a working wife," I said.

Mrs. Smonk looked at the card again. "Person to be notified in case of emergency: Mrs. Ingo Smedlo, Astoria, Queens. Relationship: mother. My guess is there's no wife."

"How about going to lunch with me, Mrs. Smonk?"

"Fine."

"Well, that's a pleasant surprise. Where shall we go?"

"I know a place," she said.

The place she took me to looked like a luncheonette from the outside. Inside was a counter with stools where high school students and welfare workers sat eating cheeseburgers and drinking Cokes. In a back room I could see a dozen elderly foreign-looking men, some with dark mustaches, sitting at tables eating. Mrs. Smonk led me into the room. The men were talking to one another in Greek. One of them nodded and smiled when he saw Mrs. Smonk. There were no other women in the room. We sat at an empty table and in a moment the man who had smiled at Mrs. Smonk got up from his table and came over.

"Mr. Andropolous, this is a friend of mine, Ross Franklin," said Mrs. Smonk.

"A pleasure," said Mr. Andropolous. We shook hands.

"There's no menu," said Mrs. Smonk. "Shall I order for us both?"

"Please do," I said.

"Want to start with some Ouzo and stuffed grape leaves?"

"Fine," I said.

The man left and returned with a bottle of clear liquor and two glasses. Mrs. Smonk finished ordering: tripe and lemon soup and spinach-and-cheese pie. Mr. Andropolous went and got the grape leaves and we ate them and drank the Ouzo.

"How much longer do I call you Mrs. Smonk?" I said.

"Call me Roberta."

"Is there a Mr. Smonk?"

"Deceased. His charming name was one of the few legacies he left me."

"And how did you come to be doing welfare work? I don't think I could take it for very long."

"I wanted to be an engineer," said Roberta, "but in those days a woman didn't have a chance unless she was phenomenal. I was only very very good. It wasn't good enough."

"Maybe you were lucky," I said. "You might have ended up making missiles for the government."

"Sometimes I tell myself that. And what did you want to do when you were young?"

"Work for Box 100," I said.

"Box 100? What's that?"

"That's where I do work. It's part of the City Department of Investigation. Anyone can write in and complain."

"And someone complained about Smedlo, or one of his clients, but either way you've got something on Smedlo."

"One woman complained about another," I said. "She may have reported her check was lost when it wasn't and then cashed both the original check and the replacement."

"It happens," said Roberta. "But it's hard to prove."

Mr. Andropolous brought the food. It was delicious.

"Now that I've been looking around," I said, "Chitty panicked and suspended the woman's case. Even if she did cheat on one of the checks, I don't see how she and her children can get along without welfare. And she's in bad shape emotionally."

"Maybe Smedlo would be willing to have her committed to Bellevue."

"Let's change the subject," I said.

"You brought it up," she said.

"I did?"

"I asked you what you had really wanted to do when you were younger and instead of telling me, you said you wanted to work for Box 100."

"Well, there was one period there where I wanted to play professional baseball—I did play semipro ball for a year. I wanted to be a writer—I worked as a sportswriter for a year. I wanted to inherit a lot of money, and an uncle left me five hundred dollars."

She smiled. "A regular story of dreams come true."

"Yes," I said. "Oh, I don't think I had any great dreams. I had a few fantasies, but I don't count those. All I've wanted to do was to move from one thing to another before I got bored and I've been able to do that, more or less."

"Never married?"

"Oh, I was married. For ten years. And I stayed at the same job for the whole time. But it was too much."

"The job or the marriage?"

"Both," I said. "But I shouldn't knock it. It was okay as far as it went. And I got a great daughter out of it. She's twenty-three now. Published a couple of books of poetry. And she's an organizer—organized some agricultural workers. You have children?"

"One. A son in California. Designs missiles for the government."

"Seriously?" I said.

"Oh, very," she said. "He's rather a bore. The job made the man, unfortunately. I guess it always does, in the long run."

"If you stay long enough," I said.

"I just spoke to him last night, in fact," said Roberta. "He calls me up regularly from Los Angeles to let me know what a mess I've made of his life. Claims I dominated him as a child. His wife's threatening to leave him again and he says I'm responsible in some obscure way. He's twenty-five years old, makes twenty-five thousand dollars a year and he has an ulcer. I get credit for the ulcer too.

"Oh, I accept my share of the responsibility for his problems. When he was a child, I thought I was exposing him to every possible avenue for the development of his own talents, but I guess engineering got exposed a little more than the rest. Children have a way of picking up very quickly what it is their parents really want."

"Naming him Wernher Von Braun Smonk may have been a mistake," I said.

"No, his name's Noel. It was a good deal more subtle than that. Still, I think his main problem is that he identifies so strongly with the missile program. Every time someone criticizes an antiballistic missile, Noel's ulcer burps. But he must be doing something right. He's got three absolutely captivating children."

Mr. Andropolous brought our check. Roberta put down three dollars to cover her part of it.

"How about dinner some night," I said.

"All right. How about tomorrow?"

"Well!" I said. "That's a pleasant surprise."

"I can be nice when I want to be."

eight

AT THREE-FIFTEEN we drove up across the street from DePasquale's grocery store. McCann was driving the truck. He was wearing his painter's disguise—a pair of stiff, brand-new bright-blue overalls and a new blue work shirt. He had carefully painted fresh spots of yellow, green and red paint on the overalls but not on the shirt, which still had sharp fold marks from its original package. A brand-new red bandanna stuck out of the side pocket of his overalls. He looked like a man on his way to a masquerade party.

The assistant district attorney, two black detectives and I sat in the back of the truck. O'Toole, the assistant DA, was a thin, red-faced, sour-looking man in his early forties who kept covering his mouth with his hand to muffle small burps. One detective, Joe Anderson, was a jovial, heavyset, muscular man, over six feet tall. He looked like a former football player, somewhat clumsy now, but exuding the calmness and physical confidence of a man who seldom encountered anything he needed to be afraid of. The second detective, Bill Holland, was a dapper little man with a goatee.

DePasquale's store had boxes of fruit and vegetables on the sidewalk outside. The rest of the groceries were inside. DePasquale stood on the sidewalk nervously pretending to be calm.

He had a long black handlebar mustache and looked like an organ grinder.

McCann wanted to go over the plan. "Now when somebody cashes a welfare check," he said, "DePasquale is going to pick up a banana."

"No shit," said the dapper detective, and both detectives laughed.

"Why not grapes?" said Joe Anderson, the big detective.

"It's too late to change the plan now, goddamn it," said McCann, getting angry.

"Okay, okay," said Bill Holland. "Quit fooling around, Joe," he said in order to mollify McCann.

"Now the first one who cashes a check," said McCann, "you watch her, Ross, and if she crosses the intersection and starts up the street toward the welfare office you say, 'I got mine.' 'I got mine' means you've picked out the one you're gonna watch. Now if she doesn't cross the intersection you say, 'No go,' and you wait for the second one who cashes a check. Once you got your suspect, O'Toole picks out one, then Joe and then Bill. You get the idea?"

We all had the idea.

"Here come some people now," said McCann. "Look at that broad. That's a welfare mother if ever I saw one."

The woman was black, very tall and somewhat overweight. But she had the kind of figure that looks—to me—even better with thirty extra pounds of fat. She wore tight fire-engine-red stretch pants and a clinging maroon sweater. Her hair was a mess. She had five children with her. She came up to DePasquale's store, picked up a bunch of bananas, gave a banana to each of her children and took one herself. Handing DePasquale some change, she started back up the street, tossing a banana peel on the sidewalk as she went.

"Shit," said McCann. The two detectives laughed at his disappointment.

"Now there's a welfare mother," said the dapper little detec-

64

tive. An elderly white woman in a shawl came up to DePasquale. She pulled an envelope from her purse, drew something out of it and handed it to DePasquale. He reached into the banana crate, picked up a bunch, looked toward the truck, waved the bananas and then dropped them back into the crate. He went inside the store and came out with some bills, which he handed to the woman. She tucked them inside her dress and crossed the intersection toward the welfare center.

"*You* take that one, McCann," said the little detective.

"Goddamn it, I got all I can do to drive and keep you clowns in line. Are you gonna give the signal or not, goddamn it, Ross?"

"I got mine," I said.

Two women cashed their checks and then went in the other direction, away from the welfare center. DePasquale was getting nervous with the signal. One woman thought he was trying to sell her some bananas. Another woman looked over at the truck when DePasquale waved a bunch at us.

Finally, O'Toole got his suspect, a poorly dressed black woman with two little boys. Then two young women came together, each cashed a check and they started toward the welfare center. McCann made a U-turn and followed them in the truck. All four women entered the center. McCann parked.

"I'm gonna look inside," he said. "You wait here. We gotta give 'em a chance to report they didn't get their checks."

He got out of the truck and started toward the building in his paint-spotted overalls. He stopped to talk to two men in front of the building—the reporter and photographer from the *Daily News*—and then entered. In a moment he came out.

"The woman with the kids is in the line for reporting lost checks. The two girls are waiting for something else."

"What about the old lady?" said O'Toole sourly.

"She's in the lost check line too," said McCann. He went back inside and was gone a little longer this time. Then he emerged again. "She's in a booth now, signing the papers," said McCann. "Let's go in."

"What about the old lady?" said O'Toole.

"She's signing papers too," said McCann.

We all went inside, including the reporter and photographer. We followed McCann over to one of the booths. The woman with the children was just coming out. McCann grabbed her by the arm.

"Okay, lady, this is it!" he shouted excitedly.

"Easy there, gangbuster," said Joe Anderson. The big detective pulled McCann gently but firmly to one side. "Let him take care of it," he said nodding toward the other detective.

Bill Holland began to speak very quietly to the woman. "We'd like to ask you a few questions," he said.

She began to cry. "My caseworker told me to do it," she said. "My kids don't have no beds. Please."

She was crying in earnest, her bosom heaving. The two little boys began to cry too, and then one of them, the smaller of the two, wet his pants.

"Those your good pants," said the woman, and the child began to cry harder. I noticed her other son had badly crossed eyes.

I heard a clicking sound behind me and realized the photographer was taking pictures. Then the little old lady came out of a booth. I looked at McCann. He saw her and looked the other way; so did the big detective.

"Bust her," said O'Toole.

Joe Anderson went over to her. "We'd like to ask you some questions," he said.

"Certainly, young man," she said in an incredibly tiny, delicate voice. "What is it?" She looked around at all of us—at the woman and her two children crying—and she began to get the picture too.

"We'd like you to come with us," said Anderson.

"All right," said the woman resignedly. "God is my witness."

When we got outside two patrol cars were waiting. O'Toole was talking to the *Daily News* reporter and also giving directions to the detectives.

"Put the old lady in the *second* car," he said in a nasty tone. To the reporter he said, "We intend to prosecute these cases to the fullest extent of the law. These are serious crimes—felonies. An offense like this undermines the whole welfare system."

Beside the first police car, the woman with the two children had gone to pieces. She was screaming and slapping the boy who had wet his pants. Joe Anderson was trying to calm her down.

"Do you need me for the rest of this?" I asked O'Toole.

"No. If I need you later I'll let McCann know."

I decided to take the rest of the day off. On the way home, instead of wine I bought a quart of gin, which I very seldom do.

nine

THE NEXT MORNING I decided to go out to Brownsville again. I toyed with the idea of seeing Mrs. Harm or Mrs. Jones. The gin had failed to put me to sleep early or kill my depression about the check raid, and this morning I was tired, sick to my stomach and had a headache.

As I entered 119 Herzl, Bumpy stopped me in the hall. He was shouting and had a wild look in his eyes.

"You goddamn motherfuckin' bastard. You got my old lady thrown off welfare! What do you care? You got all you need—you don't care how people live."

He grabbed me by the front of the jacket.

"I wasn't responsible for that," I said, not very convincingly since I didn't believe it myself.

"You're a liar! You was out here again yesterday snoopin' around, and you was snoopin' around my apartment. And now you people stole the baby and cut my old lady off. You people are tryin' to kill us."

"What baby?"

"Tito," he shouted. "What did *he* ever do to you?"

I grabbed his hand and tried to break his hold on my jacket but couldn't. He had extremely strong forearms.

"Bumpy, listen," I said.

With one hand he reached under his T-shirt and pulled out something that had been stuck in the top of his pants: a huge, rusty .45-caliber pistol. He pushed me backward, I stumbled and suddenly we were both falling. My head hit the cement and I heard an explosion like a giant firecracker going off six inches away from my ear. My whole head seemed to be ringing like a bell. Bumpy was getting back up onto his crutches, the pistol still in his hand. It was smoking. The pungent smell of gunpowder reached my nose. That was the explosion. Bumpy had fired the gun. Suddenly I felt very weak, especially my knees. I didn't think I could stand up. Bumpy rushed down the hallway and out the front door. I thought maybe I had been hit. They say sometimes you don't realize it at first. I sat there a long time waiting for something to begin hurting or for a pool of warm liquid to begin to form. None did.

I was standing in the subway, still feeling very weak, waiting for a train back to the Bedford welfare center, when I heard the screams of a child coming from the platform across the tracks. I assumed some children were playing.

The screams continued. Casually I looked across the tracks. Some children were running around, kicking at what seemed to be a bundle of rags. Then I realized they were kicking at another child. Children play rough nowadays, I thought. The screams increased in intensity and I could see that the kicks seemed to be aimed at the head of the child. Game or not, I thought, they could hurt someone. I hurried down the stairway that led over to the other platform. As I came up, five children —they looked about eight or nine years old—scampered away and a sixth, a little girl, lay on the platform sobbing.

Three adults and a teen-age boy stood staring at the girl's huddled figure. She was black and dressed in a ragged, dirty dress. They were white, and nicely dressed. I went to the little girl and bent over her. It was Willamae Jones' youngest daughter.

69

"Are you all right?" I asked.

She continued to sob and I saw blood on her teeth and gums. I took out my handkerchief and gave it to her. I touched her arm. She was not too badly hurt and I sensed she needed comforting as much as anything. I helped her wipe her mouth. Her sobs subsided a little.

"Can you stand up?" I asked after a few moments. She didn't answer, but got up. I held her by the arm to steady her.

"Are you on your way home?" I asked. She nodded. "Come on, I'll help you."

We walked past the people on the platform and they shook their heads as if to say, Isn't it terrible what those people do to one another? When I had come over to their side of the platform they had been staring at the girl as if she were an exhibit in a glass case—a pathetic exhibit, but an exhibit all the same. It just wasn't part of their view of things to break through that glass and give the child a handkerchief, or help her up. They seemed to be in their own glass case. We came out of the subway.

"Can you make it home from here?" I asked.

"They'll get me," she said, and nodded down the street. Several children were standing in a group half a block away.

"Is that them?" I asked.

"Yes."

I saw a policeman crossing the intersection, coming in our direction. I motioned for him to come over. He was a clean-cut man in his forties, with blond hair. I was relieved. Now the law could take over. The policeman had several medals pinned to the front of his blue coat.

"Some kids beat this girl up," I said. "They're down the street there and she's afraid to go home."

"You know who they are?" he said to her.

"Yes."

"Well, you and your mother can go down to the court at 120 Livingston Street and you can swear out a complaint. Do they go to your school?"

70

"Yes."

"You could go to the school and report them," he said. "It would be up to your mother."

I heard childish voices shouting curses and looked up to see the five girls advancing.

"We gonna *get* you now," said a little girl who seemed to be the leader of the group. She was all of four feet tall and wore an old yellow flowered dress that was ripped in two places, revealing ragged, dingy underwear. "We gonna whip yo butt."

"You report us and we gonna tear yo ass," said another girl.

"Come on, girls," said the policeman. "Go home."

The girls ignored him. They were standing right in front of us now.

"We gonna *kill* you, muh-fucker," said the leader.

Suddenly she rushed between the policeman and me and struck at the Jones girl, who turned away so that the blow landed on her back. I was amazed at the brazenness of the girls. I had always had a mixed feeling of fear and respect for policemen. As a child it never would have occurred to me to disregard the authority of any adult, to say nothing of a police officer.

"Go on home now," said the policeman again. I realized he was helpless and so did he. What could he do—arrest five eight-year-old girls? Even if he wanted to, they wouldn't have stood still for it.

"What did she do to you?" I said to the girls, trying to get them talking. But they ignored me too.

"You muh-fucker, we *really* gonna get you now."

The officer was clearly embarrassed by their profanity. The behavior of the girls probably seemed as foreign to him as that of Martians.

"Girls," he said, "girls."

Another child dashed in and attempted to hit Willamae's daughter, but she missed and dashed back. The policeman began to move away. "I go off duty now," he said. "Be good girls and go home."

I began to be really frightened because of my own helplessness. I could see no way to prevent the girls from renewing their beating. The leader reached past me and pulled the Jones girl's hair, and she began to cry again. Then a cab stopped for a light and I ran over and put the child in.

"Take her to 119 Herzl," I said, handing the driver a five-dollar bill.

"What is this?" said the driver. The leader of the girls jumped up and sat on his fender in an attempt to prevent him from driving off. Another opened the front door of the cab and reached in. I pulled her away.

"Lock the doors," I told the driver, and he did so. The cab moved slowly from the curb. The girl on the fender jumped off.

"What did she do to you?" I asked the girls again. Their threats to get her later worried me and I was afraid I might actually have made things worse for her.

"She always beatin' on us," said the leader. "She did this." She held out her arm and showed me a three-inch scar on the inside of the elbow.

"She had a boy do this," said another girl, who had a jagged scar on her neck just below the ear.

Now that the crisis was over I looked at the girls a little more calmly. They were dressed in old clothes. All had one or two scars on their faces and the look of having been literally battered. I had seen faces like that on skid row derelicts but never before on children.

The biggest of the girls was a lethargic-looking child who hadn't taken part in the verbal and physical assault but had merely said, "Yeah, yeah," every time one of the others cursed Willamae's daughter. A scar ran down her forehead, divided the right eyebrow into two separate bits of hair, missed the eye itself, ran down the cheek and nicked both lips. Her whole head was lopsided, as if it had been slightly mashed. She had the pimply skin of someone who subsists on Cokes and candy bars. There was a terrible hardness about the girls' faces, a terrible invulnerability. But as we talked, the fact that they were child-like suddenly came to the surface again.

"Look," said the leader, holding out a paper cup. Inside was a large snail with its two little horns. She took it out and held it in the palm of her hand. "He's mine," she said. You could see in her face the excitement of having a living thing that belonged entirely to her.

"I got one too," said another girl, holding out her cup, wanting to be noticed.

"So do I."

They all had snails.

"You gotta feed them salt and grass," said the leader.

"They're cute," I said.

"You want mine?" said the leader. "I know my father ain't lettin' me keep it."

"No—thank you," I said.

"Somethin's wrong with mine," said one of the girls.

She held it out in her hand. It lay on its back, almost limp, its stomach pulsating slightly.

"You dropped it when you were hittin' *her*," said another girl.

"Somethin's wrong with mine too," said the big girl with the terrible scar and misshapen head. Her snail lay motionless in her hand. The lower half of its body was mashed out of shape. It was dead. I realized they would all die.

When I arrived at the Bedford welfare center, I went up to Smedlo's unit. I thought he ought to know about Bumpy's gun. He was on the phone when I got there.

"Don't threaten me," he was saying in that charming style of his. "I'll get it open again. Yes . . . I *can't* see you tonight. I said don't threaten me. I don't know how long . . . Hello, hello." He smashed the phone down and then saw me.

"Goddamn it, every time I look up you're sniffing around."

"Bumpy has a gun," I said. "I thought you'd want to know. He fired it this morning in a scuffle with me."

"He fools around with me, *he* gets hurt," said Smedlo. I realized it would be just like Smedlo to carry a pistol himself, although I didn't see any bulge under his jacket.

I went downstairs to Roberta's desk. We were supposed to have dinner together.

"Hello," I said to her.

"Congratulations," she said without smiling. She unfolded a copy of the *Daily News* and tossed it across the desk toward me.

"NAB RELIEF CHISELERS," said the headline over the full-page picture. There I was, turned slightly away from the camera but still recognizable if you knew me. Beyond me in the picture was the detective talking to the crying woman. The boy with the wet pants was beside her.

"By the way, I can't make it tonight," said Roberta. "I feel slightly ill." She began to type.

I moved away and just barely succeeded in fighting back tears, which came upon me completely by surprise. I hadn't cried openly for years. I guess the incidents with Bumpy and the girls had been too much for me. And I had really been looking forward to going out with Roberta.

----
ten

I WAS AWAKENED Saturday morning by the phone. I had
been dreaming. I dreamed I was in bed with Willamae
Jones' eighteen-year-old daughter. She still had her lollipop.
Roberta was sitting in a chair across the room watching. I
was saying, "God is my witness, God is my witness," and I
was afraid to touch the girl even though I wanted to very
much.

I picked up the phone.

"Did I get you up?" It was Roberta. I thought I must still
be dreaming.

"I should have been up," I said.

"I found your number in the book. I thought you'd want
to know. Smedlo is dead. The *Daily News* says a drifter
named 'Bumpy' Jackson did it."

I didn't say anything.

"Are you there?" said Roberta.

"I don't think so," I said. "I think I'm still dreaming."

"No, you're not dreaming," said Roberta. "Look at page
fifty-two of the *Daily News*. Quote: 'Mr. Smedlo is survived
only by his mother. Reached yesterday at her home in Astoria, Queens, she said, "He was a good boy who tried to
help everyone." ' Listen," Roberta continued, "I'm sorry

about yesterday. As soon as I saw your face I was sorry. I went to look for you but you'd already left the building."

"Now I *know* I'm dreaming."

"No. In fact, I'd like you to come over to my place for dinner tonight if you can make it."

"Fine," I said.

"About seven, then," said Roberta.

"Okay," I said.

I got dressed, went to the 51st Precinct in Brooklyn and spoke to Sergeant Joe Anderson, the big detective who had gone with us on the welfare check raid. Homicide detectives had taken over the case but Anderson knew most of the details.

"A woman called the precinct," said Anderson, "and said there was a dead man in the gutter in front of 113 Herzl. A squad car checked it out and found Smedlo and they called us. I wasn't even out of my car when a big battle-ax of a woman came over and began filling my ear with this Bumpy character, how he lived in 113 Herzl and he was a wino and how Smedlo had thrown his old lady off welfare."

"A big woman?" I said.

"Yeah."

"Dressed in a long black dress?"

"Yeah. You know her?"

"I think so," I said.

"Anyway," said Anderson, "we picked up this Bumpy right away a few blocks from there. Homicide ran some tests and found out he'd fired a gun recently, and that was it."

"What's his story?" I asked.

"Claims the Mafia did it," said Anderson, and laughed. "Says he saw some guys drag Smedlo into the back of a truck, shoot him and then throw his body in the gutter and drive away. We know he's lying because he says he didn't fire a gun and the tests prove he did."

"Okay. Thanks, sergeant."

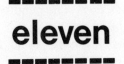

eleven

MRS. SMEDLO'S HOME in Astoria had a chain link fence around it. It was a two-family house with a tiny front yard of cement painted green. The gate in the fence was ajar. I pushed it open, went up the stairs to the front door and pushed the doorbell. I heard chimes ring somewhere inside and then a German shepherd dog came bounding around the side of the house and up the stairs, barking excitedly.

My practice with dogs and bees has been to remain perfectly still and show them you're not afraid. I was not afraid because I had never been stung or bitten. The dog snapped once at my heel as dogs will do. Then a woman opened the door and just as she said, "Down, Ralph," he snapped again, at the calf of my leg. I felt a small sharp pain, like being pinched.

"Can I help you?" said the woman. She was gray-haired and motherly-looking, with the same gray eyes as Roy Smedlo, but where his had been cold and unemotional, hers were enlivened by grief and nervousness.

"My name is Ross Franklin, Mrs. Smedlo," I said. "I'm from the City Department of Investigation. I was investigating one of your son's welfare cases. I wonder if I can come in for a minute."

"Of course. No, you stay outside, Ralph. It's all right. The man won't hurt me."

The dog growled and made a halfhearted feint toward my calf again.

"He's a wonderful dog," said Mrs. Smedlo. "He's what you call one of these attack dogs. The neighborhood has got so bad you don't know who to trust."

"I'm sure he's had all his shots," I said. I could see a tiny hole in my pants and figured the dog's teeth had broken the skin.

"Oh, yes. He had a booster just last week."

"That's wonderful," I said.

As she ushered me into the living room, I noticed she walked with a limp. We sat down side by side on a plastic-covered sofa. The room was filled with mementos of Roy Smedlo, including pictures of him at every age. Mixed in were a few religious artifacts—a plastic plaque of the Last Supper, a plastic plaque of Jesus' head with three-dimensional red drops running down from the crown of thorns.

Roy was not smiling in any of his pictures. The one on the end table beside me showed Mrs. Smedlo beaming and a five-year-old boy with a holstered six-shooter and a brand-new cellophane-wrapped teddy bear that was the same size as he was. His jaw was clamped tight and his little arm was around the teddy bear's throat in a stranglehold, the fist clenched. The room seemed as if it had always been a temple to the memory of her son, even when he was alive. The only incongruous thing was a new playpen in one corner of the room. In it was a half-full nursing bottle.

I told Mrs. Smedlo I was investigating a complaint made by one of Roy's clients against another.

"Roy was good to the colored. Too good, I guess. They didn't appreciate him. They were always pushing. They didn't realize how good they had it. Don't get me wrong. I'm not prejudiced. I rent the second floor to an Italian family. *Very* nice people. I'm just saying welfare was different in the old days. You know, Roy and I were on welfare way back and we knew how it was. You were grateful for everything you got in those days. And they could make it hard for you too. It made a big impression on Roy as a child. The investigator talked so nasty, Roy used to cry and hide when he came. The investigator always made me go and pull him out, to make sure it was really Roy, he said. I think that's why Roy wanted to work for Welfare himself—to help others."

She got up from the couch and went to a bookcase that held a twenty-volume set of the *Book of Knowledge*—undoubtedly the set young Roy used as a schoolboy—and five years' worth of *Reader's Digest Condensed Books*. She came back with a yearbook from Saint John's University.

"Roy studied sociology in college," said Mrs. Smedlo. "He was in the sociology club. He always knew what he wanted to do."

She handed me the book. I flipped through for Roy's picture. At first it didn't look as though any of the other students had signed his book. Then I came to the picture of Mary Foley, a very drab-looking girl. She had written: "Roses are red, violets are blue, sugar is sweet, what happened to you?"

I flipped through a few more pages and found another signed picture: "Best luck always, Al." The picture looked familiar. It was the owlish man with the curly hair from the Welfare Department's main office, Nolan.

I went back over the pages more carefully but didn't see anyone else I recognized. Smedlo's picture looked as if someone had told him to smile and he had tried without succeeding.

Then a baby cried in another room.

"You have a child here?" I said.

"No," said Mrs. Smedlo. She had a panicky look on her face. She realized she could hardly explain away the sound I had heard from the other room. "I mean yes. A little baby. That was just like Roy. He brought this little baby home yesterday. He wanted me to keep it for him for a few days. The mother was in trouble or something. He didn't go into it. That was just like him. He bought that brand-new playpen and some clothes. The baby's adorable. A little *colored* baby, very cute. Doesn't look colored at all. So happy, he just keeps laughing; and does he *eat* —oh my!"

"Could I see him?"

"Such a temperament. And he sleeps most of the day and all night too. Never wakes me up at night. And if he wakes up before me in the morning, he just lies in his little crib and sings to himself."

"Could I see him?"

She looked panic-stricken. "What do you want to *see* him for?"

"I might know who the baby belongs to."

"Who?" she said.

"I can't tell if I don't see him."

She led me into the bedroom and there, in a crib, was Tito.

"It's the baby of one of Roy's clients," I said.

"He didn't do anything wrong, did he?" said Mrs. Smedlo anxiously.

I didn't want to upset her further by getting onto the subject of Roy's possible transgressions. "What do you mean?" I said.

"Oh, I don't know," she said.

"Don't be concerned, Mrs. Smedlo. You have enough things on your mind now. I'll try to find out where the baby should be."

"Thank you," she said.

I walked to the front door. As soon as Mrs. Smedlo opened it, the dog came bounding up the steps.

"Down, Ralph," said Mrs. Smedlo.

The dog growled and opened his lips on one side just enough to expose one of his pointed canine teeth. My back to Mrs. Smedlo, I exposed my teeth on one side and bent my hand into a rigid claw. The dog responded by exposing all of his teeth and growling louder.

"I said *down*, Ralph," said Mrs. Smedlo angrily, and the dog moved aside to let me pass.

twelve

ROBERTA LIVED on Riverside Drive at 120th Street. Standing on the sidewalk in front of her building and looking west, I could see the Hudson River and the high-rise apartment towers on the New Jersey shore beyond. It was a beautiful, clean July evening, not too warm and with little air pollution, the result of some fluke in atmospheric conditions, no doubt. A huge red sun hung in a pale yellow sky just above the Jersey skyline.

Directly across the street from the building was Riverside Park with Grant's tomb nearby. The park was full of people. Two young men with long hair threw a Frisbee back and forth. An elderly couple sat on a park bench and looked at a book together. In the grass, a young woman was lying half on top of a young man without a shirt, kissing his shoulder.

Roberta's building was one of those pleasant, pre-World War II apartment houses in which the city had controlled the rents, keeping them low. There was a courtyard filled with green trees and pink flowering bushes; in the center was a little iron cherub standing on a little iron island that was supposed to be surrounded by water from a fountain, but the fountain apparently was not working.

I entered the lobby and pushed Roberta's bell. She answered through the intercom.

When I identified myself, she pushed the buzzer that unlocked the door. I took the elevator to the top floor. I was carrying a bag containing two bottles of fifteen-year-old Beaujolais—the survivors of a case I had bought many years before. I had been saving the last two bottles for a long time.

Roberta was wearing a beautiful dark-brown dress that made her eyes seem even more brown and a gold pin in the form of a lion's head.

"Hello," I said. She looked beautiful. I handed her the wine.

"Hello," she said. She pulled one of the bottles out of the bag. "Oh, *my,*" she said. I thought she blushed but wasn't sure.

Her living room was huge. Along one whole wall was a row of windows with a magnificent view of the park, Grant's tomb, the Hudson River and New Jersey. The room was painted a beautiful creamy gold that seemed to catch the remaining light coming in the windows. It looked as if it might have come out of a 1905 home in the Berkshire Mountains—its old American oak and pine furniture seemed to give off an air of comfort from having been used by a couple of generations of people. The copper pots and teakettles and the brass lamps and ornaments didn't have that hard, shiny look of new metal. They had a glow but it had been subdued by years of handling and polishing.

On the blond wood floor was a huge oval cowhide rug. The center was the skin of one black cow. The rest of the oval was filled with pieces of brown cowhide, and there was a three-inch border of black-and-white cowhide. From the ceiling hung a heavy wrought-iron candle holder filled with a dozen two-inch-thick white candles.

The room was saved from being entirely a period piece by a huge semiabstract painting on the wall opposite the windows, of an Indian wearing an elaborate headdress. The canvas was filled with violent reds and yellows and oranges.

"I could stay in here forever," I said. The room made me feel at peace, but it was an odd thing to say and I thought hard for another quick remark. There was a delicious smell in the air. "What's cooking?" I said.

82

"That's not dinner," she said. "I want a few drinks first and I like to eat a little when I drink. Come on into the kitchen and I'll show you."

Like the living room, the kitchen was huge. In the center was a heavy old table whose wood was scarred from the slicing of meats and vegetables. From a wrought-iron rack suspended above the table hung copper kettles and ladles and spoons, a skein of red onions, a heavy old-fashioned salami and a string bag of lemons and limes. There was a pan of hot fat on the stove and a pitcher of batter with a funnel beside it.

"Funnel cakes," she said. "Want to try?"

"Of course."

"But let me mix a drink first," she said. "I'm on a Margarita kick at the moment. How about you?"

"Fine," I said. "But before too long I want to switch over to that wine."

"You open it then," said Roberta, "and we'll let it breathe."

She squeezed lemons and limes and mixed two very large Margaritas. Then she took the pitcher of batter and poured some into the funnel, putting her finger over the small end so the batter wouldn't run out. She held the funnel over the pan, removed her finger and let a rope of batter run into the simmering fat. She moved the funnel quickly back and forth so the batter crossed over itself several times and ended up in the shape of a crazy pretzel. She made two of them. They browned almost at once, like doughnuts, and in about two minutes they were ready.

Roberta took them out of the hot fat and put them on some paper towels and then on a plate, and we carried them into the living room. We sat on a couch looking out the windows toward the Jersey shore. The sun was touching the horizon now and the sky was a brilliant yellow. The funnel cakes were hot and just slightly sweet.

"Out of this world," I said. "Forget supper; I'll have these. Did you invent them?"

"It's an old Pennsylvania Dutch recipe, made out of corn-meal, eggs, butter and sugar. I didn't get a name like Smonk without a few fringe benefits."

We sat in silence for a while. The Margarita was making me relax, and the funnel cakes and the sunset were giving me a sense of the goodness of some things.

"So," said Roberta finally. "The world turns. Smedlo gets it, after all these years of giving it out. And some poor wino spends the rest of his life in Sing Sing. I don't know which is worse."

"Dying can only turn out one way," I said. "There's no way of knowing how Sing Sing might turn out."

"Yes. It might be charming. Like getting raped by a prison gang, for example."

"That's true," I said. "I have a tendency to keep forgetting things like that."

"Don't we all," said Roberta.

"Whatever you may think," I said, "I really would like a job where nothing I do causes anyone else to get kicked in the face."

"Who got kicked in the face now?"

"Well . . . *you* know," I said.

Roberta reached over, took my hand and squeezed it. "I'm sorry for the way I acted yesterday."

"I was thinking about Smedlo too," I said. "The man they're holding is the boyfriend of the woman I told you about. If I hadn't been looking around, the case might not have been closed and Smedlo might not have been killed."

"I think his luck just ran out," she said. "I wanted to kill him myself a couple of times."

"I met Mrs. Smedlo," I said.

"What is she like?"

"She and Roy were on welfare when he was a kid," I said. "Roy used to run and hide when the investigator came because he talked too nasty to his mother."

"That happens sometimes," said Roberta. "The kid grows up trying to be like the people who seem to have the power."

"There's a baby in the picture too," I said. "Tito. He belongs somewhere in the Jones family, although Mrs. Jones denies it. Smedlo took him to his mother's house on Thursday and he's still there."

"My God," said Roberta. "It gets more complicated by the minute."

We finished our drinks. It was almost dark now outside, and inside, too, since we had no lights on.

"Another funnel cake?" Roberta asked finally.

"Definitely. And a little of that wine."

Roberta made two more funnel cakes, I poured two glasses of wine, she lit the candles in the wrought-iron candle holder and we settled on the couch again.

"This wine is marvelous," said Roberta.

"I'm glad you like it," I said. The Margarita had loosened my tongue and I talked more than I should have. "It brings back memories," I said. "I had a case of this wine. I drank the rest of it five years ago with another lovely woman. She left me. She needed someone with a more settled life, but she never found him. I found out recently that she killed herself."

"It's stupid for me to say this, Ross," said Roberta. "Maybe the liquor has made me stupid—but the memory of time spent with a woman like that is better, in some ways, than the memory of ten years of a dull marriage going slowly nowhere."

"You must be a mind reader," I said. "The month that woman and I had together was worth whole years from other times in my life. The only trouble is, months like that are not really life. Life is ten years of a poor marriage. Life is a job like the job I have now. Months like that are drama, not life. They're scenes out of a play called 'How I'd Like My Life to Be.' Sometimes you get a five-minute scene—a really perfect five minutes. Sometimes you get a whole month at a time. But you add it all up and out of a life of sixty years, what does it come to? Nine months? Twelve? Eighteen? With her it was that perfect first month of a relationship before ordinary life takes over from drama. It was a little bit like the last two hours."

We looked at each other and then kissed. Then we held hands and looked out the window a long time. We drank some more wine. The lights from the candles flickered on the walls. Roberta's head came to rest on my shoulder. I closed my eyes.

The next thing I knew, birds were chirping somewhere. I was in a dark room. A woman was lying half on top of me and my arm was around her. Roberta and I had fallen asleep. The candles had burned out. Outside in Riverside Park, birds were chirping. It looked dark but the approaching sunrise must already have been lightening the sky in the east.

Slowly my eyes became accustomed to the dark. Roberta was still sound asleep. She slept like a child. Her face was peaceful. She was breathing softly through her mouth. Her breath was sweet. She looked beautiful. I tried not to move, but before long the strain of remaining still became too great and I shifted slightly. A small frown appeared on Roberta's face. "No," she said. She snuggled her face more comfortably on my chest.

The birds increased their chirping outside. Now I could see the sky getting lighter. In the darkened apartment towers across the Hudson, lights began to come on. I shifted again slightly.

"Stay," murmured Roberta. I could feel the warmth of her breath through my shirt. Then she woke up. "Where the hell am I?" she said. Then, making a quick recovery, she said, "Well, are you ready for dinner?"

"Just about," I said. I realized I was very hungry.

"Good morning," said Roberta. She gave me a long, slow kiss on the mouth. "Let me make you coffee and bacon. It's a ritual of mine." She got up. In about three minutes the aromas of coffee and cooking bacon drifted into the living room. I went out into the kitchen and put my arms around Roberta from behind as she stood at the stove. She turned her head back and we kissed again.

Later Roberta cooked the steak she had planned for dinner the night before, and I made my specialty, bananas in hot rum and brown sugar sauce. Sitting on the couch, we ate and drank some more wine, watched the apartment lights come on in the towers across the river and listened to the birds and the milkman. It was very domestic in a pleasant way, not at all mundane but the way domesticity ought to be.

Roberta lent me a razor and I shaved. We spent the morning reading the Sunday *Times* together, then packed a picnic lunch and ate it in a densely wooded area of Central Park that few people apparently knew about. Later we went to an exhibition of the paintings of Georgia O'Keeffe at the Whitney Museum.

At dusk we returned to Roberta's apartment. Before starting to make supper, she went into the bedroom and changed into some lounging pajamas.

"I like to be comfortable," she explained.

"How about me?"

She went back into the bedroom and brought out some men's pajamas and a robe.

"Try these," she said.

When I came out of the bathroom with them on, supper was almost ready. We kissed again.

Awakening on Monday morning, I discovered that Roberta was already in the kitchen fixing the coffee and bacon.

Halfway through breakfast the spell was broken when a stiff breeze developed from the west and blew in a wave of air from New Jersey that smelled exactly like stale cat urine. The resemblance was uncanny.

"Am I dreaming," said Roberta, "or is that . . . ?"

"Cat urine," I said. "They must bottle it in Jersey some-where."

"My God, what next?"

"Well, let's see," I said, trying to think of the possibilities.

"Never mind," she said.

We kissed good-bye at the door of her apartment.

"Call me at work during the day," she said.

thirteen

I WENT FIRST to the lobby of my apartment building to see if there was any mail. I found a letter from Willamae Jones in the box.

Thank you for what you done for my doter. Bumpy say to see him. Hes sorry he fite you. He need help bad. Sincere Willamae Jones.

I called up Joe Anderson, the detective at the precinct, to find out how to get in to see Bumpy. He told me he would call the city prison, where they were holding Bumpy, and speak to Lieutenant Gregoria, who was in charge of the case.

"We're still looking for the weapon on that case," said Anderson. "It's a thirty-eight."

"A thirty-eight?" I said. "Are you sure?"

"Yeah, why?"

"No reason," I said. I hung up. The gun that Bumpy had pulled on me was a forty-five.

Lieutenant Gregoria was waiting for me at the city prison. He was a good-looking man with black hair, a black Fu Manchu mustache and blue eyes.

"I understand you know this man," said Gregoria.

"Yes."

"Do him a favor, tell him to wise up. We have him nailed. If he'll admit it and tell us where to find the gun, we can probably work out a plea of second-degree murder. If *we* find the gun, he can forget about a plea. He's gonna get life."

"I'll tell him what you said."

In the visitors' room I looked at Bumpy through a glass slot in the wall and spoke to him by phone.

"I didn't do it, Mr. Franklin," he said. "It's a frame-up. The police might be in on it themselves. They're not even investigatin' the clues I gave 'em."

"What clues?"

"Like the reflector from the truck."

"What reflector?"

"The Mafia was in a truck," said Bumpy. "Two of them got out to talk to Smedlo. They wanted him to get in with them and he didn't want to. They opened the back door of the truck and threw him in. He was kicking and he broke one of the red reflectors at the back of the truck. After they threw him out of the truck I picked up the pieces in the street."

"What makes you say it was the Mafia?"

"They had on navy-blue shirts and white silk ties."

"Bumpy, you can't expect the police to believe a story like that."

"Because they're in on it."

"It just sounds like the kind of story someone in your position would make up," I said.

"Smedlo was carrying city welfare checks when they killed him and I can prove it."

"Even if you could, I don't see what that would tell us."

"It would tell us he was a crook too. I found three checks on him. Willamae is holdin' 'em for me. I wrote down the names." He held up a small piece of paper on which three names were written: America Acevedo, Carmen Acevedo, Tammy Acevedo. "Write these names down," said Bumpy. "This is an important clue."

I copied the names on a small piece of paper and put it in my pocket. "I know what this'll prove to the police," I said. "It'll prove that you robbed Smedlo after you killed him. I haven't told them about your pulling a gun on me, but I'll have to."

"Do you know what kind of a gun I pulled on you?" he asked.

"A forty-five," I said. "Why?"

"Because Smedlo was killed with a thirty-eight."

"I know," I said. "So maybe it would help you if they knew you had a different kind of gun. That would explain where the powder burns on your hands came from too."

"They're not gonna listen to no one. They're in on it."

"Listen," I said. "I promised Gregoria I'd tell you that if you plead guilty they can arrange a second-degree-murder charge."

"Shit," said Bumpy. "Even my Legal Aid lawyer's tellin' me to do that, but I ain't doin' it."

"Okay, Bumpy."

"I don't expect you to believe this either, Mr. Franklin, but that forty-five went off by accident. I didn't even know it was loaded."

"God knows why, Bumpy, but I do believe you," I said.

The guard came and took Bumpy back to his cell.

Gregoria was waiting outside. "What'd he say?" he asked.

"He said, 'Shit.' Listen, lieutenant. On Friday Bumpy pulled a gun on me, and while we were struggling it went off."

"Why didn't you tell me that before? Come on into my office. I want to get a statement on that."

"It was a forty-five-caliber pistol," I said.

"What kind of a pistol?" he asked. He had suddenly become extremely cold.

"A forty-five," I said.

"How do you know it was a forty-five?"

"I know what a forty-five looks like, lieutenant."

"Most people don't," he said.

"I do."

"Did you discuss this with him in there?" he asked.

"If you mean did we make it up, no."

"You'd testify under oath that it was a forty-five?"

"Of course," I said.

"If what you say is true," said Gregoria, "then he had *two* guns." Apparently he had lost interest in taking a statement from me. "I'd like you to bring the clothes you were wearing when the pistol was fired down to my office for some tests."

"Look, lieutenant, why should I make up a story to protect Bumpy?"

"I don't have the slightest idea."

"Lieutenant, do you have some pieces of a truck reflector?"

Gregoria laughed. "No, we gave them back to the Mafia."

"Can I see them?"

"What we have is a few pieces of red glass like the kind you can pick up in any gutter in the city."

"Can I see them?"

He called to someone to bring Bumpy's belongings. In an envelope was an old, worn wallet, some keys, the ebony carving of a clenched fist on a rawhide cord, and eight pieces of red glass. I laid them out on a desk and tried to put them together like the parts of a puzzle. I played with them for a moment and then arranged them in a circle with one long V-shaped piece missing.

"Big deal," said Gregoria. "Listen, Franklin. So far this year I've worked on seventy-six homicides. You know how many were done by people like Bumpy?"

"Eighty-five?" I said.

fourteen

WHEN I GOT OFF the elevator on the way to my office I ran into José, the guard.

"Congratulations, Ross," he said. "I want you to autograph that picture for me."

"What picture?"

"The *Daily News* picture."

"José, I'm not too proud of that."

"Don't say that, Ross. You're a hero around here. Pat had Xerox copies made."

"Oh, Christ. José, did the woman in that picture look like a criminal?"

"She looked kinda shady to me, Ross."

When I got to my office, I found a copy of the photograph taped to the wall near my desk.

"Hey, Ross," said McCann. "You made it."

"Yeah, I made it," I said. "Good morning, Laura."

The papers came up to cover her face.

"No telegram from the mayor yet?" I asked.

"No," said McCann, "but we got another case for you. A blind lady that's been cheating on welfare."

"Fabulous," I said. "My kind of case."

"Wait till you hear the whole story. She's collecting welfare at half a dozen centers. I gotta run now, Ross. Got another appointment with those chippies. You're fifteen minutes late and you lose your turn and you gotta pay anyway. Here's the letter on the blind woman. They sent a photograph too. Personally, I doubt if she's really blind. We also got a letter from Mrs. Harm with a complaint about you. She says you don't seem to care if people cheat or not. . . . Your attitude really shows, Ross."

"Yeah, I guess it does. Maybe I can redeem myself on this blind lady's case."

The East New York welfare center, where the blind woman was supposed to have one of her many cases, looked almost exactly like the Bedford welfare center. A long line of people stretched down the block and around the corner. Two hundred or so more people were milling around inside.

"Is it always like this?" I asked the receptionist.

"No, never," she said. "It looks like half the neighborhood didn't get their checks. Usually we have half a dozen lost checks for zip code seven. Look at the list today."

She turned the sheet of paper around so I could see it:

Aaron, Walter
Abalen, Willie
Abner, Johnnie
Abrams, Joyce
Acedo, José
Acosta, Maria
Aguilar, Octavia
Ahern, Mabel
Albert, Barbara
Albright, Florence
Alers, Manuel
Alexander, Roy
Alison, Joan
Allen, Carol
Alleva, Maria

Alston, July
Alvarez, Carmen
Amor, Phillip
Anderson, Ruby
Andrews, Shirley
Borden, Ralph
Donaldson, Sharon
Hughes, Ellen
James, Roy
Jones, Pearl
Norris, Plessy
Ralph, Ardelle
Smith, Billie
White, Carol

"Hmm. That's interesting," I said. I took out the picture of the blind woman and showed it to the receptionist. "Did you ever see this woman in here?"

"Sure. That's Rosie. She's blind. Mr. Hastings handles her case. There he is over there, talking to that old man." She pointed to a red-haired young man with bushy sideburns.

When Hastings finished talking to the old man, I went up to him.

"Excuse me. My name is Franklin, from the City Department of Investigation. The receptionist tells me you're Rosie's investigator." I showed him the picture.

"Yeah," said Hastings. "What'd she do?"

"I don't know that she did anything. Do you have her last name and address?"

"Her name's Rosie Morris and she lives at 1357 East New York Avenue. I visited her there last week. What's it all about?"

"It's just a routine check. How long has she been on welfare?"

"About two months."

"Thanks," I said.

I went from the center to 1357 East New York Avenue, a two-family house that had been broken up into a rooming house. In front of the building a man with a hose was cleaning the sidewalk.

"Does Rosie Morris live here?"

"The blind lady?" he asked.

"Yes."

"When she's around she lives here. She's not here much of the time, but I think she's up there now."

"What room number?"

"Top floor, 4R."

I went up and knocked on the door. There was no answer but I heard someone moving around inside. I knocked again.

"Go away," said a voice from inside.

"I want to talk to you," I said.

"Go away," the voice repeated.

"I have to talk to you."

There was no sound from inside. I waited two minutes, then knocked again.

"Go away," said the voice, which now spoke from just inside the door.

"No," I said. After waiting another two minutes, I said, "Mrs. Morris, I must talk to you."

"How do you know my name?" she said.

"Someone told me. Can I talk to you for just a minute?"

"You talkin', ain't you?"

"Can we talk face to face?"

"Face to face don't mean nothin' to me. I can't see no face."

"I'd like to see you though, Mrs. Morris."

The door opened four inches. A chain prevented it from opening farther. It was the woman in the picture. She was a black woman with five prominent warts on her face, three on her forehead, one on her left eyelid and one on her chin. Behind her I saw the kitchen. Canned goods, boxes of cereal and cookies and loaves of bread were scattered on the table, on the refrigerator, on chairs, in the sink and on the floor. Loaves of eight different kinds of bread were lying opened on the floor by the door. On the kitchen table was a mound of canned goods two feet high.

"Mrs. Morris," I said, "what is all that food for?"

"To eat," she said.

"Mrs. Morris, there's enough food for ten people in there."

"I need somethin' to eat when they throw me off welfare like they done before."

"Mrs. Morris," I said, "some of that food is spoiled." I saw roaches scampering over a box on the floor containing a half-eaten layer cake. "There are roaches on it."

"I don't hear no roaches."

"Okay, Mrs. Morris, thanks for talking to me."

"You a fool. Don't know nothin' 'bout welfare. Ask me why I got food. I bet you're white, ain't you?"

"Yes."

"I knew it. You prob'ly the one tryin' to get me thrown off welfare."

I left the building.

fifteen

OUTSIDE THE BEDFORD WELFARE CENTER there was an even longer line than at the East New York center. Inside, I could hardly get through the crowd. I went up to the receptionist. "What's going on?" I asked.

"It seems like twice as many people as usual didn't get their checks this time."

I showed her the picture of the blind woman and asked if she'd ever seen her.

"Yes, she's a client here. I don't know her name, but Mr. Frank was down here talking to her this week sometime."

I went up to see Frank, a blond-haired, hazel-eyed man who was wearing a light-blue shirt and a red, white and blue necktie.

"Yeah," he said when I showed him the picture. "That's Maybell Brown. What's the problem?"

"No problem," I said. "Where does she live?"

"At eighty-six Herzl."

"May I have a look at her case record?" I asked.

"Help yourself. It's on my desk. But don't blame me for what happened to that woman. Until last week it was someone else's case."

I took the folder and went into the office I had used before. After I had been looking through it for fifteen minutes, Valjean Wilcox came in.

"Hi," she said.

"Hi," I said. "Have a seat."

She sat down. "Well, Smedlo won't get the prize," she said.

"No," I said, "unless we give it to him posthumously. People may love him more now that he's gone."

"Yeah, pos'mously, or whatever you said. I know I can dig him much better where he is now than when he was sitting at that desk out there. I can tell you one thing though," she added. "Bumpy didn't do it."

"There's only one way you could know that for sure, Mrs. Wilcox," I said, meaning if she had done it herself, a possibility I didn't take too seriously.

"Two ways," she said. "Suppose Bumpy was with me when Smedlo was killed?"

I love people whose minds work that fast. "If he was with you," I said, "why didn't he mention it to me or to the police?"

"Maybe we don't want to play all our cards until we see what you people have."

I felt she was bluffing, although I knew she was quite capable of lying in court if she wanted to help Bumpy badly enough.

"What else is new?" she said, when I didn't reply.

"Nothing much," I said. The last thing I wanted was for her to know I was working on the blind woman's case.

"Aid to the blind?" she said, noticing the markings on Maybell Brown's case record.

"Damn it, Mrs. Wilcox, do you always have to be so observant?"

"It's Miss Wilcox," she said. "Now that's what I was talking about. Just because I'm not married doesn't mean I don't have a man or some kids. And if my name was *Mrs.* Wilcox, it wouldn't mean I *did* have a man. Half the married women in the ghetto don't have a steady man. I doubt you'd understand the reasons why."

"Try me," I said.

"Later. But take me, now. I *don't* have a steady man right now, but I want a kid in the worst way. I could be a good mother

99

to a kid now. Before, I just wasn't ready. So now I'm trying to adopt one but your adoption agencies are giving me a hard way to go because I'm not married. I guess they'd rather have the kids stay in one of their crummy overcrowded institutions. You're white, your people run those institutions and those adoption agencies; maybe you can figure it out."

"Well, look," I said, "I have other problems right now."

"Yeah," she said. "What did the blind lady do—have an illegitimate child or something?"

I blushed.

"You don't have to be embarrassed, Mr. Franklin," she said. "I know you're only doing what you have to do. It's nothing new to us. It's what we're used to. We've been watching white folks from the back of the bus all our lives."

She refused, even for a moment, to give up her insistence that because she was black and I was white we were in two absolutely separate worlds, and it made me angry.

"Oh, for Christ's sake, Wilcox, you never rode in the back of a bus in your life."

"No," she said, and suddenly her expression became so hard that it was almost painful to look at her. "I never did. My father told me what it was like, and that was worse. My father told me what it was like when he was a fully grown man to have a five-year-old white boy say to him, 'John, bring me my boots.' What do you suppose that kind of thing has done to our men?"

She stood up to go. I wanted to ask her to stay but I didn't know what words to use. I just couldn't bring myself to apologize to her for what some five-year-old white boy had done to her father thirty years ago. I believe she wanted to stay. Instead neither of us spoke as she opened the office door, stepped out and closed it behind her.

I took the blind lady's case record with me and went up to see Roberta.

"How's it going?" she asked.

"Fabulously," I said. "Now I have a blind woman who has at

100

least two cases open simultaneously and she may have even more."

"You can't excuse cheating just because she's blind," said Roberta.

"Thank you, Dr. Norman Vincent Peale. I don't excuse it because she's blind. But let me give you a little bit of her background. Before she got welfare she had a boyfriend with a disability pension from World War II and they made a little extra money making deliveries and trips in an old 1952 Nash Ambassador. They could earn a buck or two taking people to the clinic or the hospital or get a free slab of government-surplus cheese for helping an old lady home with her bundles from the surplus-food depot. But then, during a cold spell, the radiator block on their car froze because they couldn't afford antifreeze. At first they were turned down when they applied for welfare. The Welfare Department seems to operate on the assumption that if you can't prove how you got along before, you can't get welfare now. They didn't know the names of the people they took to the hospital or brought home from the surplus-food depot. The investigator said they had to have statements in writing from the people that gave them food or money, and not many people would give them statements. People didn't want to get involved with the Welfare Department.

"So while they were trying to convince the investigator that they really had survived the way they said, they got evicted from their apartment. I guess that convinced the Welfare Department that they didn't have any money, because they opened the case. The boyfriend wanted the Welfare Department just to open a case for the woman—he said he could live on his disability check and didn't want welfare. But they made him give half his disability check to her and they both ended up on welfare. And somehow there was less money for him that way than if he just kept his check and she got welfare, so he left her and stopped giving her half of his disability check. Without that money she couldn't pay the rent and she got an eviction notice. Listen to this. Quote: 'We explained to Mrs. Brown that we have no intention of paying her rent until she brings in proof that her boyfriend is no longer residing with her and giving her money.' I don't know how she was supposed to prove it. Anyway, the Welfare Department didn't pay her rent and she got thrown out. Maybe that was the proof they wanted; I don't know.

"After she got thrown out, they seemed satisfied that he was really gone, and eventually she got another place to stay. Then someone wrote an anonymous letter that she had a boyfriend living with her. Two days later, at six A.M., her worker and a special welfare investigator and a policeman banged on her door and made her open up. Sure enough, there was a guy with her, an alcoholic with three fingers missing who had been in and out of state mental hospitals for years. I don't know exactly what they wanted from her, or from him for that matter, but they cut off her check and she went through the same thing again. She says, 'The boyfriend is gone'; they say, 'Prove it'; she says, 'How?'; they say, 'That's your problem.' So she gets thrown out of her apartment for the third time and somehow that seems to prove the boyfriend is gone. Or maybe that's her punishment. Anyway, she's smart enough not to have another boyfriend. Just to make sure, they break in on her a couple more times, but they don't find anything."

"What happens to her now?" said Roberta.

"Well, I want to check some more centers to find out if she has more than just these two cases."

"Then what happens?"

"I'll think about that later."

Suddenly Chitty dashed up to Roberta's desk.

"What's the trouble on that Brown case?" he said. He seemed almost in a panic.

"No trouble," I said.

"I know her case," he said, a little more calmly. "She's been a troublemaker ever since she first started getting welfare.

When you're through with that record, I'll go over it to see if I can find any hanky-panky. You know, there's a rumor going around that you were here investigating Smedlo."

His tone was friendly now compared to the hostility he had shown last week. "I wanted you to know I'm going over all his cases with a fine-tooth comb and I'm making a list of everything that looks at all questionable. For example, before he left on Friday—before he was killed—he prepared the Willamae Jones case to be reopened. Don't you think that's suspicious?"

"No," I said.

"Well, my supervisor, Mr. Longley, does. *He* wants to see my whole list. Smedlo was sending a lot of money to Mrs. Jones' daughter Willette too, and that's very strange for him."

Chitty turned around and flounced away from the desk.

"By the way," I said to Roberta, "I talked to Bumpy Jackson this morning. His story is that the Mafia killed Smedlo."

"That's as good a story as any," said Roberta. "They're getting blamed for everything else. Listen, I have a surprise for you— Mrs. Smedlo's old welfare folder."

"You're kidding," I said.

"No."

"They kept it all this time?" I said.

"Welfare never forgets a case," she said. "After you told me the family had been on welfare I called Central Records Storage and sure enough, they had the case and they sent it over. It's fascinating. Apparently Ingo Smedlo, the father, was a very hard worker. He managed to find menial jobs through most of the Depression but his luck ran out in 1937 and he couldn't find any work. Or maybe he just got tired of shoveling scrap iron for twenty-five cents an hour. That was his last job. He began to drink and finally, when there was no alternative but welfare, he deserted. Mrs. Smedlo claimed he couldn't face the welfare people. He had the guts to clean toilets in Pennsylvania Station but he didn't have the guts to face the bureaucrats, and maybe he was right. When Mrs. Smedlo tried to get welfare they told her that Ingo was probably sneaking back to see her and so she ought to know his address. She claimed she hadn't seen him and didn't know where he was. They made her get a warrant for his arrest for nonsupport, and then they still wouldn't give her welfare. Finally Roy stole some food from the neighborhood grocery store and when the police came to see Mrs. Smedlo about it she jumped out of a second story window and broke both legs."

"My God," I said.

"The more things change, the more they remain the same," said Roberta. "By the way, this might interest you." She handed me a typewritten list of names. "These are the clients in zip code twelve who reported that they didn't receive their checks this time, and the list is twice as long as usual."

I looked at the list.

> Acevedo, America
> Acevedo, Carmen
> Acevedo, Tammy
> Ackley, Simon
> Acosta, Esther
> Acuna, Maria
> Adams, Marjorie
> Addison, Virginia
> Aguilar, Carlos
> Aguinaldo, José
> Alexander, Willie
> Allen, Christine
> Alvaredo, Pedro
> Alvarez, Maria
> Ambrose, Willette
> Ames, Esther
> Anderson, Mabel
> Andrews, Carol
> Austin, Earlene
> Ayala, Verna
> Brown, Grace

Cummings, Lila
Douglas, Joan
Franklin, William
Graham, Paula
Harvey, Georgette
James, Edwina
Moore, Florence
Robertson, Ora
Thompson, Ruth

"This is odd," I said. "It's top-heavy with names beginning with *A*. I was over at the East New York center and it seems to me their list was like that too. I can't understand why it would be that way. Is there another center you can call and see if there's anything funny about their list of checks?"

"Sure. I'll call Shirley at the Queens center." She picked up the phone and dialed. "Shirley? It's Roberta. . . . Fine. . . . Do me a favor, will you? Look at your list of checks reported missing. . . . It is?" She covered the receiver and spoke to me. "She says the list is twice as big as usual and it's happening at most centers in the city." She spoke back into the receiver. "Shirley, is there anything funny about that list, like a lot of names beginning with *A*? . . . No?" Roberta shook her head at me. "It is?" she said into the phone. "No kidding. Our list is top-heavy with names beginning with *A*. Okay, Shirley. Thanks." She replaced the receiver. "At her center half the names on the list begin with *M*."

"Can I have a copy of your list of checks?" I said.

"Sure. Here." She handed me one of the onionskin copies.

"I think I'll go down to the main office and ask some more questions," I said. "It'll take my mind off Maybell Brown for a while. I'll call you later."

I left the center and headed for the subway.

sixteen

WHEN I GOT to the main welfare office I went directly to Dombrow's office. His secretary stopped me.

"He's awfully busy," she said.

"This is awfully important," I said.

"Just a minute." She picked up the phone and buzzed Dombrow. "Mr. Franklin is here again. He claims it's important." She hung up. "You can go in," she said.

As I opened the door, Dombrow was just closing the middle drawer of his desk. There were no papers on the top of it.

"Mr. Dombrow," I said, "twice as many clients as usual are at the welfare centers saying they didn't get their checks."

"Tell me something I don't know," he said.

"I just wondered if you had any idea why."

"Yes, I know exactly why. Twice as many clients are pretending they didn't get their checks. They want a second helping."

"Oh, really? You seem to know everything else, Dombrow— maybe you know why half the people who lost their checks in zip code zone twelve had names that begin with *A*."

"What's that, a riddle?"

I handed him the list.

"Coincidence," he said.

"It was the same in zip code seven at East New York. At the

Queens center, on the other hand, half those with missing checks had names that begin with *M.* Talk about a coincidence, Dombrow—this seems more like a miracle. Do you suppose the good Lord is trying to suggest it's time to change the system? Maybe he's sending us a message in code."

"Very funny," said Dombrow.

"Yes. If it's not an act of God," I said, "I have an alternative hypothesis."

I opened my wallet and took out the little slip of paper on which I had written the names of the people whose checks Smedlo was carrying when he was killed. I compared it with the list of missing checks from Roberta's center. Smedlo's checks belonged to the first three people on Roberta's list.

"What are you doing?" said Dombrow as he watched me compare the three names with Roberta's list.

"Dombrow," I said, "can you show me how the checks get sent out?"

"Yes." He got up and I followed him out of his office and down the hall to a door marked "No Admittance." There were two locks on the door. Dombrow took out his key ring and opened both. We went inside and he locked the door behind us. Along one wall was a huge bank of computers.

"These are the brains of the Department of Welfare," said Dombrow.

"Yeah," I said. "I knew you were hiding them somewhere."

Dombrow gave me a dirty look. He ignored my remark and continued his explanation. "I keep the key to these machines on my person at all times."

"That figures," I said. "PYA, right?—protect your ass."

"That's right," said Dombrow. "Twice a month I turn these machines on and they print almost half a million checks. The checks for each zip code in the city come out together, in alphabetical order. The machine puts a band around every twenty checks."

We walked over to one of the machines.

"Bundles of checks come out here," said Dombrow, pointing to a large square opening in one of the machines. "The machine also makes a record of every check it prints. It's called a printout. The printout for Thursday's checks is here in this basket."

"Can I see Thursday's printout for zip code twelve at the Bedford center?" I asked.

Dombrow went to one of the computers, leafed through the printout and showed me the list of checks sent out for zip code twelve. I took Roberta's list and compared it with the printout. "The first twenty checks printed by your machine for zip code twelve are all missing, Dombrow. Every single check. One complete bundle. Now what do you suppose explains that?"

"The post office must have fucked up again," said Dombrow. He had lost his usual composure and it was the first time I had heard him use profanity. But he still had an answer for everything.

"The post office?" I said.

"Yes," said Dombrow. "When the checks come out of the machines, we put them in those bags over there, a few bags for each zip code, and then we lock the bags."

"We?" I said.

"Nolan and I."

"By the way," I said, "where is Nolan today?"

"Why?" said Dombrow.

"I'm just asking."

"He's not here," said Dombrow.

"Where is he?"

"Franklin, I don't like your insinuations."

I decided not to pursue the subject of Nolan any further. "Okay," I said. "Forget Nolan. You put the checks in the bags and lock the bags, and then what do you do?"

"Nolan watches while a couple of laborers take the bags down to a truck and then he rides in the truck and they deliver the checks to each post office."

I went over and looked at the bags the checks were put into.

108

They were made of heavy wire mesh covered with burlap. If anyone cut open the bags, it would be noticed immediately.

"Who has the keys to those bags?" I asked.

"I have a key for each bag," said Dombrow. "And each postmaster has the keys for the bags for his zip code."

"Where do you keep your set of keys?" I asked.

"You must be stupid, Franklin. I told you I operate on the PYA principle. You don't think I'm going to take any chances with these checks, do you? I keep the keys to those bags locked in my desk." He pulled his key ring out of his pocket. "And the key to my desk stays in my pocket at all times."

"I didn't notice you locking your desk when we left," I said.

"That just proves you're stupid. You'll find it's locked."

We went back to Dombrow's office. "Go ahead and try it," he said.

It was the kind of desk we had at the Box 100 office and the same kind they had at the welfare centers—gray metal with a gray plastic top. You had to open the middle drawer before the drawers on either side could be opened, and there was a lock on the middle drawer. For the first time I noticed a small number stamped into the lock. The number on Dombrow's lock was 253. Making a mental note of the number, I tried the middle drawer. It was locked.

"Satisfied?" said Dombrow.

"Yes," I said. "Just out of curiosity, may I see the keys to the mailbags?"

"Don't worry, Franklin, they're in there."

"May I see them?"

Dombrow unlocked the desk and took out a key ring containing several hundred keys. He shook them at me as one would shake a rattle to amuse a baby.

"Dombrow," I said, "how many people reported they didn't get their checks this time?"

He picked up the phone. "Gloria, what's our total of checks reported missing?" There was a pause and then he put the phone down. "Eight thousand four hundred and forty-four."

"Three thousand lost checks on the first of the month and eight thousand on the seventeenth of the month," I said. "That's quite a jump, isn't it? Five thousand extra checks missing this time. At two hundred bucks a check, that's an extra million dollars in checks that's missing."

"Out of a total yearly budget of one point four billion dollars, one million dollars is chicken feed," said Dombrow.

"If you say so, Dombrow. And your theory is that those five thousand missing checks are most likely missing because each of the two hundred post offices in the city fouled up—a mass foul-up involving every office in the city."

"Listen," said Dombrow. "I mailed an airmail special delivery letter to my sister in Los Angeles and you want to know how long it took to get to her? Seventeen days. So don't tell me about the post office."

"Dombrow," I said, "just in case someone has managed to steal a million dollars' worth of welfare checks, is there any way you could stop payment?"

"Of course there's no way. But it's not necessary. If someone in the post office stole those checks, he'd have no way in the world to cash five thousand of them. Who's gonna cash five thousand welfare checks?"

"I don't know," I said. "If I find out, you'll be one of the first to hear."

seventeen

ON THE STREET outside the Welfare Department's main office I picked up a copy of the late edition of the *Daily News*. "BUST GAL FRIDAY FUN RING," said the headline. The picture showed seven policemen accompanying five girls and two men out of a building. The caption said, "Police arrest secretaries and customers in alleged lunch-hour play-for-pay ring."

I looked at the picture again. One of the men was covering his face with his hands. He had on a loud Hawaiian sport shirt. It was Pat McCann. The story didn't mention anyone by name.

I went back to the office and was in the middle of writing a report on what I'd found out so far about the blind woman when the phone rang. It was Pat.

"Look, Ross, I'm in a little jam. I've got fifty bucks in an envelope in my desk, and I need it. Now don't tell anybody, but I'm down at the city prison. It's a case of mistaken identity, but I'm locked up down here and I need the fifty bucks to get bail money. It's in the middle drawer of my desk."

"Okay, Pat," I said. "I'll be down in about half an hour." I hung up. I didn't have the heart to tell him about his picture in the paper.

When I tried Pat's middle drawer I found it was locked.

"Laura, do you have the key to Pat's desk?"

"No. He wouldn't trust me with it."

"Well, I have to get something very important for him. Do you think Cooper would have a key?"

"No, but I know how to get a key."

"How?"

"There's a locksmith in the basement for all the city agencies in the building. All you have to do is find out the little number on the lock and go down and tell the locksmith. See that little number right there?"

On the lock on Pat's middle drawer was the number 204.

"Want me to go down to the locksmith?" said Laura.

"No," I said. "I'll go."

At the elevator I met José.

"Hey, Ross, did ya see where they smashed a play-for-pay ring down on Canal Street?"

"Yes, I saw that."

"Ross, there's a guy in that picture with a shirt like Pat's." José looked worried.

"Maybe he was doing undercover work, José," I said.

"Wow!" said José.

I took the elevator down to the basement. A sign directed me to the locksmith shop. Inside I found a kindly, grandfatherly-looking little man with white hair and wire-rimmed glasses.

"We need the key to one of our desks up at Box 100," I told him.

"What's the lock number?"

"Two hundred and four."

Behind him were rows and rows of nails driven into a board on the wall. Each nail held about ten keys. He ran his finger down the rows. "Here it is," he said. "One key be enough?"

"Yes," I said. "How many desks do they have in this building?"

"They have about a thousand but there are only three hundred and twenty different locks. This way, the chances are that all the desks in one area will have different locks."

"You have keys to all the desks here?"

"Sure. We have to. On the average, three people a week lock themselves out of their desks. One week in 1967 I had eleven lockouts."

"Can I get a key for lock number two fifty-three?" I asked.

"Sure. One key be enough for two fifty-three?"

"Just to be safe, why don't I take three?"

"There you go," he said. He slipped the keys into a tiny brown envelope and handed them to me.

I went upstairs, opened Pat's desk, found the money and took a cab to the city prison. Once I got there with the money, Pat was out in fifteen minutes. On the way out of the building, Pat picked up a *Daily News* someone had left on a bench.

"Oh, shit," he said when he saw the picture. "You think anyone would recognize me?"

"You, no; the shirt, yes. José already spotted it. I told him maybe you were doing undercover work."

"That's *it!* I wanted to see if there were any city workers involved. Thanks for everything, Ross. I want to go back to the office and figure out exactly how to explain this to Cooper."

Pat went up the street toward the subway. Passing him from the other direction was Joe Anderson, the detective from the precinct. He was carrying a package in his hand.

"Hey there, Franklin," he said. "Say, what'd you say to Gregoria this morning?"

"Why?"

"He really cursed you out. I called him about an hour ago to tell him we found a thirty-eight pistol in Jackson's neighborhood."

"You found a thirty-eight?"

"Yeah. Here it is," he said, indicating the package. "Now we have to test it to see if it could be the weapon that killed Smedlo."

"How long will it take to trace the owner?" I asked.

"We did that. It was registered to Ophelia Harm. She's the one who first tipped me off about Bumpy Jackson. She claims she dropped her purse near the stoop one day when Willamae Jones' daughter was loitering there. A little boy brought the purse up to her door later but the gun was gone. That's her story. It doesn't quite add up. When we found the murder weapon was a thirty-eight we went back to the neighborhood to ask people to keep an eye open for it. I talked to Harm myself and she didn't mention losing her thirty-eight."

"How long will it take to find out if this is the murder weapon?"

"Well, you can never be perfectly sure. It's not like fingerprints. What we'll find out is if it *could* be the gun. Or the tests might rule it out altogether. We should know late tomorrow. Our analyst has gone home already and Gregoria doesn't think it's worth putting him on overtime. Gregoria's sure it's the gun."

Anderson continued on his way and I walked to the subway. I was tired now, and didn't try to figure out the significance of the gun. I just wanted to pick up a bottle of wine and get to Roberta's apartment. I stopped at a good liquor store in her neighborhood and asked for a bottle of Catawba Pink wine.

"We don't have it," said the proprietor, a stocky, balding man who let his sideburns grow long to compensate for the absence of hair on top.

"Gee," I said, "it's a very nice rosé—better than that Portuguese rosé you have there."

"We don't have much call for it in this neighborhood. I stock it in my other store, in Harlem. Mostly it's the colored that drink it."

"Well," I said, "I wonder if you could order me a case."

"Ordinarily I'd be happy to oblige," said the man, "but with that particular item I can't help you." He leaned closer, lowered his voice and spoke confidentially. "I can't afford to let my customers think I cater to the colored, you know what I mean?"

I had lost my taste for wine. What I needed now was a tall glass of gin on the rocks. I remembered that Roberta had an unopened fifth in her cabinet. I left the store.

eighteen

ROBERTA WAS HOME when I got there.

"What's for supper?" I said when she let me in.

"I thought I'd let you decide."

"That's nice," I said.

"Yes," said Roberta. "After all, since you're making it, why should I decide?"

I laughed. I went into the kitchen and opened the refrigerator.

"Let's see," I said. I pulled out a pot of leftover beef stew, and jars of leftover peas and leftover onion soup. "A shot of burgundy and a dash of oregano for the beef stew," I said, throwing them in and putting the pot over a gas flame. "A shot of sherry and a dash of garlic for the soup." They went in, and I poured the soup into a pot and put it on the stove. "A shot of vermouth and a dash of pepper for the peas."

"That's cheating," said Roberta. "What would you do without the leftovers?"

"Did you ever have burgundy, oregano, sherry, garlic powder, vermouth and pepper on the rocks? Delicious. Instant supper."

She laughed.

"My only other specialty is roast suckling pig, and it doesn't fit most occasions."

"Try me sometime," she said.

"I will," I said, and made a mental note to cook a pig to celebrate our first week together. We ate the leftovers by candlelight and it seemed like a banquet. My desire for a tall gin on the rocks was gone.

nineteen

THE NEXT MORNING I called the central welfare office and asked for Nolan. I was told he hadn't come to work again. I looked up his home phone number and dialed it. After it had rung a few dozen times I hung up. I decided to go to his home. As I walked up the street to the subway I had to pass the liquor store where the man refused to stock Catawba Pink wine. It was about eight o'clock and he wasn't open yet.

A black man reading a newspaper was leaning up against the store's protective metal gate, as if waiting for the store to open. He was wearing a big, bright-red golf cap and yellow slacks.

After I had been on the subway platform for about a minute the man came through the turnstile just in time to get on the train with me. I took the subway to East Flatbush in Brooklyn, where Nolan lived. The address I had got from the phone book was a one-family house. No one answered the doorbell. There was no sign of life inside.

I rang the bell of the house next door. A blond woman in pin curls and a bathrobe answered the door.

"I'm trying to locate Al Nolan," I said.

"They've been away for the last three days," said the woman. "I saw him and his mother get into a taxi with suitcases on Friday night."

I went back to the subway station and got into a train to Manhattan. Just as the doors began to close, the man with the red golf cap and yellow pants squeezed in the door, shot a look in my direction and then went to the other end of the car and pretended—or so it seemed to me—to study his newspaper. He was wearing large sunglasses and had his hat pulled low so I could not see his whole face.

A slight twinge of fear went through me. I couldn't think of any reason why someone should be following me. I thought, Maybe I'm just paranoid—maybe he isn't following me. Just as the doors were closing at the next station, however, I impulsively got up from my seat and slipped out of the train. It was too late for the man to get off. As the train pulled out of the station I thought I saw him watching me through the window.

Up in the street, I took a cab back to the main welfare office. When I got to Dombrow's office, he was standing at his secretary's desk trying to answer the phone. He pushed one of the five buttons on the phone and barked, "Hello," then pushed another button and again barked, "Hello," but the phone kept ringing. "The hell with it," he said, and slammed the receiver down. The ringing continued. "That damn woman is always sick. What the hell do *you* want?" he said to me.

"I take it you know Nolan has skipped town," I said in an attempt to make him a little more cooperative. For all I knew, Nolan and his mother might be on a much deserved vacation. But it produced the desired effect. Dombrow seemed to weaken before my eyes. He plumped himself down into his secretary's chair.

"He has?" he asked. He made another try at answering the telephone, which was still ringing. He picked up the receiver, pushed a button and very meekly said, "Hello." The phone kept ringing. Gently he set the receiver down again.

"How do you *know* he skipped town?" he said. He was not a man who was used to being vulnerable. His nerves couldn't take it. That may have been why he was so concerned about protecting his ass. I took the little brown envelope from the locksmith out of my pocket.

"Dombrow," I said, "here are three keys to your desk." I held out my hand with the keys in the palm but he didn't reach for them. He looked stunned. One by one I laid the keys down on his desk. He stared at them. He picked one up and inserted it in the lock. He unlocked and locked the middle drawer. Then he picked up a second key and looked up at me. The key dropped out of his hand back onto the desk. I almost felt sorry for the man. Whatever was going on inside him wasn't pleasant to look at.

Suddenly his face flushed to a beet-red color. Even his ears began to turn red. Then he stood up, leaned across the desk and with his right hand grabbed my shirt and tie at the throat. He was also pinching some of the skin of my neck. He began to shout and twist the fistful of skin and cloth. I felt a sharp pain at my throat and found I couldn't breathe. I had been pulled across the desk toward him and was off balance. I couldn't get my feet under me enough to struggle. Lack of oxygen was already making me weak. The arteries near my eardrums were pounding. Dombrow's voice sounded like it was coming from a great distance. "What are you insinuating? Huh? What are you insinuating? What are you insinuating?"

Some memories of childhood began to rush through my mind —jumping off a henhouse roof and almost poking my eye out with a sharp stick; going into the hospital to have my tonsils removed and getting a book with a reindeer on the cover as a reward; running down a high-school hallway and smashing into the six-foot-tall woman who taught English. My mind told me that Dombrow must be choking me to death because my life was flashing before my eyes like they always said it did. But it wasn't the way I had imagined it would be. It wasn't your whole life at all, just episodes. Even while I was having these thoughts, the episodes from my life continued too—getting drunk and sick at a wedding reception for my best friend; hitting a triple

in the last inning of a championship baseball game and dying
on third; making love to Olivia, the woman who had killed
herself.

A man's face was peering down at me. "You're not supposed
to lie down in here." I closed my eyes. I felt as though I was
going to faint. The collar of my shirt seemed to be choking me
and I reached up to tug at it. When my hand touched my throat
I felt a sharp pain. My neck was swollen and sore. I rested a
minute. Then I loosened my tie and unbuttoned the top button
of my shirt.

"Jesus," said the face, which was still peering down at me.

"What?" I said.

"Your throat is all black and blue and purple. It makes me feel
sick to my stomach to look at it."

"Don't look at it," I said.

"Let me help you," the man said, and began to tug me into
a sitting position. All I really wanted was to lie where I was and
rest for a few moments. Once he had me in a sitting position,
he tried to pull me to my feet by bending over and lifting under
my arms. When my buttocks were six inches off the floor the
man lost his grip and dropped me. My spine jarred on the floor
and my head flew back and hit the wall. I almost lost consciousness. I sat there, half slumped against the wall, closed my eyes
and rested.

"I think I strained my back," said the man.

I opened my eyes. He was sitting in Dombrow's chair clutch-
ing his back. I tried to think of something humorous to say, but
nothing came to mind. I rested a while longer and then sat up
straight. My head cleared a little. I got to my feet unsteadily.

"Jesus, my back," said the man.

I left and went back to the Box 100 office.

twenty

COOPER WAS SCREAMING at Pat McCann when I arrived.

"Don't investigate any so-called *leads* unless someone writes us a *letter* about it, and don't go poking into anything unless I know about it."

"Okay, chief," said Pat. "I only did my duty as I saw it."

"Well, *don't* do your duty as you see it. Do your duty as *I* see it." Cooper turned to me. "And *you*," he said. "Who asked you to go to the main welfare office and investigate lost checks?"

"Who asked you to impersonate a human being?" I said.

McCann looked at me, wide-eyed with disbelief. I'd had almost enough for one week and it was only Tuesday morning. Still, it was too soon to quit. I wouldn't even get my first pay check until Friday and I wanted to buy a pig to cook for Roberta.

"What did you say?" said Cooper through gritted teeth. I could see him clenching and unclenching his jaw muscles. In a strong man that gesture is sometimes impressive. In a man like Cooper it was amusing. It looked like he was exercising to build up those muscles so he could chew his food more thoroughly. And he knew perfectly well what I had said. But since he was giving me an opportunity to say it again, I decided to be conciliatory.

"I said, 'What makes you such an impersonal human being?' "

Cooper liked the second version better. Apparently he didn't feel up to a big scene with me right after his big scene with Pat.

"I'm not impersonal," he said, "but I don't let my feelings interfere with the job. Did you talk to a man named Dombrow?"

"Yes," I said.

"Well, he says you assaulted him. What the hell is going on, Franklin?"

"He assaulted me," I said. I loosened my tie and opened my collar. "See this?" I thought my wounds would establish me as the victim.

"Jesus!" said Cooper. "You *did* assault him! You're off this case, Franklin! Everything is going to be handled by the district attorney's office. You stay in touch with this office by phone at all times. Leave a number where you can be reached in case the DA has any questions. They think someone in the post office stole five thousand checks."

"There would be two hundred different post offices involved," I said, "and you'd have to have a thief in each one."

"You don't think there's at least one crook in every post office?" said Cooper.

"All working together?" I said.

"Look," said Cooper. "Listen. Let the DA worry about the post office."

"Gladly," I said.

"And I want a progress report by this afternoon on that blind woman's case," said Cooper.

"Gladly," I said. "Gladly, gladly, gladly, gladly."

Cooper looked at me as if I had lost my mind. I hadn't but I was beginning to understand what it feels like when you do.

twenty-one

I WENT TO TWO more Brooklyn welfare centers and found that the blind woman had had cases at each for about three months. I visited the two different home addresses she had given and heard the same story from tenants at both of them: the woman had an apartment in the building but was seldom in it. I knocked repeatedly on the door of each apartment, but there was no answer.

The address the woman had given Roberta's center was 86 Herzl, which turned out to be a run-down apartment building like the others. The name Maybell Brown was on the mailbox for apartment 1A. I knocked on the door and heard feet shuffling inside.

"Mrs. Brown," I called. The door shot open. The woman with the warts on her face stood in the doorway and behind her stretched a long hallway piled high with cans, boxes and bags of food.

"Is that you again?" she asked. "You won't be satisfied until I'm dead, so why don't you kill me?" She ripped her dress open and exposed one breast. Two of the buttons from the dress fell on the floor. "Kill!" she said. "Kill! Kill!"

I realized now what was going to happen to her. After having been evicted at least three times in her life so far, she was going to have all of her cases closed and be evicted again, not once, but one by one from every apartment she had accumulated.

"I'm sorry, Mrs. Brown," I mumbled, and left the building with cries of "Kill! Kill! Kill!" following me into the street.

twenty-two

ON MY WAY down Herzl to the subway, a voice called my name.

"Mr. Franklin!"

It was Mrs. Harm.

"Hello, Mrs. Harm."

There was a look of near contentment on her face such as I had never seen before. "You look as though you're in a good mood," I said.

"Good enough," she said. "I told you Smedlo were gonna get his reward. I had a feelin'."

"Yeah," I said. "He got his reward with your pistol."

"That Jones girl stole it from me."

"So maybe the police are holding the wrong person," I said.

"I thought of that," said Mrs. Harm, "but if she done it, Bumpy most likely knowed about it and when he gets closer to the 'lectric chair he'll think twice about tellin' someone."

"They don't have the electric chair anymore in New York, Mrs. Harm."

"That's too bad, but when he gets closer to the reformatory he'll tell what he knows."

"Why would the girl kill Smedlo?" I asked.

"I don't know," she said, "but there were something funny goin' on between Smedlo and the Joneses. They say Smedlo stole that baby from Mrs. Procacino. She's all confused about it, but someone saw a white fella comin' out of that house with a baby on Thursday night. Maybe that's why they killed him. Maybe Smedlo killed the baby."

"No," I said. "He's all right. How much do you know about Tito, Mrs. Harm?"

"Well, it began funny. 'Bout three years ago Willette, the daughter, was supposed to be pregnant. Least that's what some people claimed. But she went down south for six months, so no one knew for sure. Goin' down south made it look kinda suspicious though. And when she came back, natcherly, she didn't have no baby with her. Then 'bout a year and a half ago Mrs. Jones, the mother, got pregnant. Seemed like Bumpy was the father. She had the baby at Kings County Hospital but she came home from the hospital without the baby. Claimed he had some kind of condition they had to fix up before she could take him home. She went back a week later to get him. But it was funny, no one saw the baby for the first six months they had him home. They hardly ever brought him out. That's all I know. I don't pay no attention to what go on over there."

"Okay, Mrs. Harm. Thank you."

She went on down the street. I wondered whether things would fall into place more clearly if I understood the puzzle about the baby. Since I was so near, I decided to go and see Mrs. Jones.

When I got to the door of her apartment, I found it open about four inches. I knocked.

"Come in," said a voice somewhere inside the apartment. It sounded like Willette. I pushed the door open, stepped into the empty living room and closed the door behind me.

"Mrs. Jones?" I called. The apartment was quiet. Across from me a door opened into the living room. Willette stood there in the doorway, barefoot and wearing her old green silk robe tied loosely at the waist. The robe was open at the top and her beautiful full breasts were more than half exposed. They bobbed gently as she came toward me.

"Mr. 'vestigator," she said. She was very much self-possessed. She studied my face carefully. "Why you want my mama?" she asked. "You don't think I can take care of you?"

I knew I should get out of the apartment but I stayed so Willette wouldn't realize how nervous I was. At least I told myself that was my reason for staying. Willette came up to me and stopped with her breasts two inches from my shirt. She touched one of my shoes gently with her bare foot. I forced my face into a cold expression but I had the terrible feeling that the strain of trying to look calm was giving me away.

"I'm hot," she said, and reached down and untied the bathrobe, brushing my pants with her hand in the same gesture.

"Come on, Mr. 'vestigator, you know you want it."

She was right. At the same time that I was appalled by her utterly self-composed, calculating approach I was stirred by her beautiful body and the odor of her cheap lilac perfume, a scent to which I have always been embarrassingly susceptible.

I was about to touch her waist when, over her shoulder, I saw her little brother, the four-year-old with the Afro hairdo, standing in the doorway to the kitchen. He smiled a happy smile and said, "Hi!"

Willette turned toward him. "Go back in the kitchen, Gabriel. Can't you see we're busy?"

He retreated into the kitchen, but the spell was broken. My hand was on the front doorknob now. As I opened it, I said, "Willette, I'll come back when your mother's home."

I opened the door and stepped out, but before I could close it I saw Mrs. Jones coming down the hall with the other three children, including the girl I had tried to help in the subway.

Mrs. Jones tried to smile when she saw me but it ended up being half a smile and half a wince. "Hello, Mr. Franklin."

"Hello, Mrs. Jones," I said. "Can I talk to you for a few minutes?"

"Come in," she said. "You was lookin' for me?"

"Yes."

As she stepped into her apartment she saw her daughter leaving the living room in her robe and her face twitched. She looked from her daughter back to me, but she was too nervous to search my face for a sign of what might have happened. Even though nothing had, it had come so close that I felt guilty. To ease her nervousness, I wanted to tell her, "Nothing happened," but I didn't have enough courage to bring it out into the open.

"I want to thank you for helpin' my daughter in the subway," said Mrs. Jones.

"That was nothing," I said.

"Is there anythin' you can do to help Bumpy?" she said.

"I don't know," I said. "I'll have to try to understand a few things better before I can figure out what I can do for Bumpy. I want you to know Tito is all right. He's with Mrs. Smedlo, Smedlo's mother."

Her face twitched and a tremor seemed to go through her body.

"I know that Tito belongs here," I said. "You don't have to pretend with me. I don't understand why you didn't want Welfare to know that Tito belonged here."

"Smedlo said not to mention Tito," said Mrs. Jones.

"Why would he say that?" I asked.

"I don't know," said Mrs. Jones. She was beginning to tremble now.

"Whose baby is Tito?" I said.

"Bumpy's and mine," she said.

"Do you have a birth certificate?" I said.

Relieved to get away from me, she went and opened a drawer that was filled with papers. She looked through them for a moment and then pulled out a black photostat of a birth certificate. Her hand shook as she held it out to me. The mother was listed as Willamae Jones, the father as Andrew Adelbert Jackson and the child's name was Malcolm Adelbert Jackson. According to the date of birth, the child would have been one year old this month.

"Thank you," I said, handing the certificate back to Mrs. Jones. "So the child's legal name is Jackson."

"Yes," she said.

"You know," I said, "Mrs. Harm claims that Willette probably took her gun, the one that was found in this neighborhood yesterday."

"That woman so full of hate, she prob'ly killed him herself," said Mrs. Jones.

"But Bumpy claims it was the Mafia," I said.

Mrs. Jones winced.

"It *was* the Mafia, if Bumpy say so. But if it weren't the Mafia, it were Mrs. Harm."

"Mrs. Jones," I said, "I wonder if I could look at those welfare checks Smedlo was carrying when he was killed."

She got up again, went to the edge of the room and lifted the linoleum. The checks were underneath, laid side by side. She picked them up and brought them over to me. They were still in their mailing envelopes, which had not been opened. The names were exactly as Bumpy had given them to me: America, Carmen and Tammy Acevedo.

"Thank you very much," I said. I got up to go. "Mrs. Jones, I want you to know nothing happened in here before you came."

She looked away as I opened the door and stepped outside.

I was anxious to make some phone calls, but I didn't find a pay phone that worked until I got to the subway station. First I called Kings County Hospital, where Malcolm Adelbert Jackson had been born one year before. Tito, I was sure, was at least two years old. Mrs. Harm had mentioned that Mrs. Jones came home without the baby and then went back and got him a week later. I wanted to know the discharge date for Malcolm.

"That baby was never discharged," said the lady in the records room at the hospital.

"How can that be?" I said.

"Usually it means the baby died. Let me look through the death certificates for that week." There was a pause. "Here it is. He died a week after he was born. 'Congenital heart defect,' it says here."

"Thank you," I said.

Next I called the precinct and spoke to Joe Anderson.

"Yeah," he said. "They did tests on Mrs. Harm's gun. It couldn't have been the gun that killed Smedlo. It hadn't been fired for years. Gregoria almost had another stroke. This case is gonna give him a hernia of the brain."

Finally I called Roberta at the Bedford center.

"Pat McCann from your office has been calling here every fifteen minutes trying to find out where you are," said Roberta. "I told him we were supposed to have lunch together but he says your boss wants you back at the office. He says it's urgent."

"Okay, Roberta," I said. "If he calls again, tell him I'm on my way to the office now. I should be there in about forty minutes. I'm at the subway now. I'll try to get back out for a late lunch with you too, okay?"

"Fine," she said.

"Around two?"

"Good," she said. "How are you, Ross? You sound hoarse."

"I've had better days," I said. "I was nearly strangled by the head of the Welfare Department computer section. I have a tendency to get a sore throat from that sort of thing."

"Are you sure you're all right?"

"Yes," I said.

"He had something to do with the missing checks?"

"I doubt it, Roberta," I said. "If he'd had something to do with it, it wasn't logical for him to attack me when he did. He attacked me when I proved to him that someone else could have got into his desk. That's the only thing that seemed to disturb him, and it would have let *him* off the hook as far as the missing checks are concerned. His main commandment is to protect his ass, and he attacked me when I showed him his pants were down. But I think I figured out whose baby it is that Smedlo's mother has."

"Don't tell me, let me guess—it's obviously Smedlo's."

"I think so. I think Mrs. Jones' daughter is the mother. She went down south about two and a half years ago when the rumor was going around that she was pregnant. When she came back she didn't have a baby, but then her mother got pregnant, and she claims Tito is her baby. The only trouble is her baby died in the hospital of a congenital heart deformity. Tito is a year older than her baby would be anyway."

"They went down south and brought the daughter's baby back as a substitute," said Roberta.

"I think so," I said.

"Why did Smedlo take the baby to his mother's?"

"After Chitty forced him to close the Jones case, Willette may have threatened to expose Smedlo as the father, so he stole the evidence. No baby, no paternity proceedings."

"So maybe Tito killed Smedlo," said Roberta. "When he found out what kind of a guy his daddy was."

"That theory makes as much sense as the Mafia," I said. "By the way, it wasn't Mrs. Harm's gun that killed Smedlo."

"I'm betting on Tito and/or the Mafia," said Roberta.

"Okay, Roberta. See you for lunch."

twenty-three

I SAT in the subway car and tried to forget Box 100. I was sure they wanted me back at the office to find out what I had learned about Maybell Brown, and I didn't want to tell them. But I wasn't ready to quit the job until I got paid on Friday.

I had to figure out how I was going to stall Cooper about Maybell Brown. Should I just lie, and claim I hadn't found out anything yet? Then he might fire me before Friday. Maybe Cooper would understand the logic of leaving one of her cases open so she'd have one apartment and something to live on.

The train pulled into a station and a man got on who looked familiar, but I couldn't place him. He sat down directly opposite me. He was in his thirties, was over six feet tall, burly looking and expensively dressed. His big head was covered with curly black hair that came down over the back of the velvet collar of his chesterfield-style jacket. He had pale hazel eyes that were almost yellow, and bushy black eyebrows that met in the middle. He wore a pair of metallic-rimmed "granny" eyeglasses.

Somehow I connected him with Smedlo. He carried a huge, expensive briefcase which he held tightly on his knees with both hands as if it were very valuable. He looked over at me for a moment as if he was on the point of remembering me, then the thought passed from his mind, and he pulled some kind of a list from his inside breast pocket and studied it. Instinct told me to get up and move away a little so he wouldn't recognize me. I changed seats and reached inside my jacket for my horn-rimmed reading glasses to use as a disguise. Just as I put them on, I remembered where I had seen the man before—it was when I had run into Smedlo and the call girl outside a nightclub the week before. This man, and another woman, had been with Smedlo and his companion.

When he got off at the next station, Atlantic Avenue, I did the same. It was the first time I had ever followed anyone in my life, and in spite of all the detective movies that make it look easy, it was not. I was afraid I would lose him if I let him get too far ahead, and that he would recognize me if I got too close. I worried about one and then the other as I moved closer and then dropped back and then moved closer.

He walked briskly down the street to a bank and went inside. I stood outside and watched him through the window as he got into one of the lines. A *Daily News* was lying on the sidewalk so I picked it up to use as a prop. I was nervous. I pretended to be reading the newspaper while I watched him. Really seeing the newspaper for an instant, I found I was holding it upside down. When I looked around to see if I had attracted attention to myself by holding the paper that way, I saw the man with the bright-red golf cap and yellow pants. He was standing about ten yards away appearing to examine a store window. He was looking at me out of the corner of his eye.

Again I felt a twinge of fear. Now I was absolutely sure he was following me. If you know why someone is following you that's one thing; but to be followed by a stranger when you have no idea of the reason is another matter. When you're involved in a case where a man has been murdered, and you don't know by whom, or for what reason, it's all the more upsetting. For the first time, I wished I was carrying a weapon.

I looked back into the bank to see what the other man was doing. He was up to the teller. I couldn't determine what kind of transaction was taking place. As he walked away from the teller I thought I saw him shove something into his briefcase and then he came toward the front door.

I looked around outside and found that the man with the red cap had disappeared. I didn't want to be standing near the bank door when the other man came out so I began to walk up the sidewalk away from the bank entrance, looking over my shoulder as I went. The man came out of the bank and began to walk behind me. Now he was following me. As I tried to catch a glimpse of him reflected in a shop window I bumped into a woman.

"Why don't you watch where you're going?" she said indignantly.

Suddenly I saw the man enter another bank, which I had already passed. I walked back to the entrance, but there was no window I could look into. I went inside. He was standing in a line marked "Checking," holding three checkbooks. He looked at the first two, then stuck them in his pocket and began to make out a check in the third. I stood on his line. There were five people between us. When he got to the window, he ripped a check out of the book and handed it to the teller. A short conversation took place, the teller referred to his files, then he pushed a small pile of bills through the window. The man went over to one of the desks along the wall, opened his briefcase and put the bills inside. Then he walked out of the bank.

I got out of line, left the bank and followed him again. He walked ten blocks, then entered another bank. I went in too. He made his way to one of the desks along the wall, opened his briefcase, took out two checkbooks, put one back in the case and got on line. I let someone else get behind him and then I joined the line.

He wrote out a check and when he got to the teller pushed it through the window.

The teller consulted his records and then came back to

the window. "This will leave only five dollars in your account," he said.

"Is there anything wrong with that?" said the man.

"No."

"Then what's the problem?"

"There's no problem. But this is a very large amount. Two thousand dollars. Maybe you'd like a bank check or traveler's checks?"

"No," said the man. "Cash."

"All right," said the teller. "I'll have to get it. I don't have that much in my drawer. How would you like it?"

"Five-hundred- or thousand-dollar bills, if you have them."

The teller was gone for about two minutes. The people in the line had the usual exasperated expressions of those who get stuck behind a man with a fancy transaction. They looked mournfully at the other lines, which were moving faster. When the teller came back, he pushed a few bills through the window. The man took them, went over to one of the desks by the wall, took a heavy manila envelope out of his briefcase and put the bills in it. He put the envelope back inside the case, closed it and walked to the revolving door. I hurried too much in trying to keep up with him. As I entered the door he glanced back and looked straight into my face. He frowned a little. He remained by the revolving door, about two feet from where I would have to emerge. It was too late to do anything about it; someone was pushing the door behind me.

I decided to pretend I had forgotten something inside the bank and stayed in the revolving door. He was still watching me and I saw his frown deepen as I continued back into the bank. My pretense wasn't very effective. Apparently it resembled the Marx Brothers more than Humphrey Bogart.

When I got inside, I looked out the front window and saw the man stepping into a cab. I rushed back to the revolving door, but two people were in front of me. By the time I reached the sidewalk, three cabs were moving up the street and there was no way to tell which one the man had entered. I returned to the bank and went up to the teller who had taken care of the man. The people in the line glared at me, thinking I was trying to get ahead of them.

"Listen," I said to the teller. "I need to know the name of the man with the curly hair who cashed a check for two thousand dollars."

The teller looked at me with a shocked expression. "We can't give out that kind of information."

"I'm with the New York City Department of Investigation," I said. "This is official business."

The man looked skeptical. The people on the line behind me seemed to share his attitude.

"Do you have any identification?" he asked.

I wished I had accepted Pat McCann's offer of a Jersey City police department badge.

"No," I said.

"You'll have to have your supervisor send a letter to our main branch," he said.

"Look," I said, "this is extremely important."

"Do I have to ring for our security man?" said the teller. He looked for support to the people on the line behind me. Their indignant expressions matched his. I got out of line and left the bank.

As I stepped outside, the man in the yellow pants was facing me. His red cap was pulled low over his forehead and he still had on his sunglasses. Before I could even figure out what to do he said, "Franklin, you sure are a jive investigator."

I was momentarily disoriented. The voice was as familiar to me as Roberta's, and yet I couldn't place it. And it had a femi- nine lilt to it. He took off his glasses. It was Valjean Wilcox.

I was furious—at her for fooling and scaring me and at myself for being fooled and frightened by her. I exploded: "Goddamn it!"

She began to laugh uproariously, which made me all the more angry.

"What the *hell* do you think you're doing?" I demanded.

"I'm trying to pick up a few pointers about detective work. I'm getting tired of being a case aide. How would you like a partner? It looks like you could use a little help."

"In an outfit like that?" I said.

"I don't *have* any dull clothes. Is that what you recommend? Dressing dull didn't seem to help you too much. That dude sure gave you the slip."

"Wilcox, you're hilarious," I said without smiling.

"Call me Valjean," she said.

"No, thanks," I said. "Too familiar. Black people don't like to be called by their first names. It's a carry-over from slave times."

She laughed. "Whatever you say, Ross." It was the first time she had called me by my first name. I couldn't help smiling.

"I'm going to take your advice," she said, "and go buy some inconspicuous clothes." She turned as if to leave. "By the way," she said, "is it very important to you to know who that man is that you were following?"

"Yes, it is, Valjean, but I really would appreciate it if you'd leave it to me. I get paid for it; you get paid for being a case aide."

"Okay," she said. "If you change your mind, though, give me a call, because I know the dude."

She turned and began to saunter away. I immediately dismissed my first reaction—that she was bluffing—because I was getting to know this woman and knew it was dangerous to call her bluff. I swallowed my pride and started after her.

"Wilcox," I said.

"Valjean," she said, and grinned.

"Valjean," I said, "do you really know who he is?" It was a stupid question to ask because I already knew the kind of answer she would give me.

138

"Mr. Franklin—" she said, and I interrupted her.

"Ross," I said, and we both smiled.

"Yes, Ross," she said, "I know him."

"Who is he?" I asked.

"Is he involved in the stolen checks?" she asked.

"What stolen checks?" I said. She knew enough already and I didn't want to tell her any more than I had to.

"*You* know, Ross. Like those three checks Bumpy took from Smedlo." She paused. Then she smiled and added, "And like a few thousand more that haven't turned up yet."

"He may be," I said.

"Him and Smedlo, right?"

"Maybe, Valjean, maybe. Now are you going to tell me who he is?"

"He's Nick Kowalski, the son of that crooked mover down on Schermerhorn Street. I met him at his father's office a couple of times before I stopped using them to move my clients."

"Kowalski?" I said. Now it was time for me to play my game. I didn't want her to know I had ever heard of the Kowalskis. "Where on Schermerhorn Street?"

"I'm sure it's in the phone book," said Valjean. "I can't remember the address."

"To tell the truth, Valjean," I said, lying through my teeth, "I don't honestly believe there's any connection between Smedlo, these moving people and the missing checks. It seems pretty likely that the checks are still in the mail somewhere because of a foul-up by the post office. I hate to disappoint you. I'm more interested, right now, in that blind woman's case. She's getting welfare at four different centers."

"More power to her," said Valjean.

"Yeah," I said. "The black approach to the welfare problem, right?"

"Right on," she said. "Give us what's ours—give us jobs,

schools, decent apartments, and you can keep welfare. But if all you're gonna give us is welfare, don't complain when we take it for all it's worth."

"Okay, Valjean. Now be a good girl," I said, "and go back to the welfare center and read some case records."

"Don't call me 'girl,' " she said. "People might think you're prejudiced."

"I'm old enough to be your father, dear," I said.

"You're so square, Ross," she said. "Age doesn't make any difference. My daddy was forty-seven when he had me, and my mother was the same age I am now."

I blushed.

"See you later," she said, and started walking in the other direction.

twenty-four

I DECIDED to go immediately to the office of the Kowalski Brothers. When I got off the subway I called Roberta again from a phone in the station.

"McCann is calling every ten minutes now," said Roberta. "He says an assistant district attorney wants to talk to you. Aren't you going to get into trouble for not going back?"

"I think I'm onto something, Roberta. I'm on my way to Kowalski Brothers, the movers. If I'm right, I don't think I'll be in trouble— Better not wait for me for lunch, though."

When I got to 126 Schermerhorn I wasn't sure what to do. I decided to check the back alley to see if there was a fire escape to the second floor, where Kowalski Brothers had their office. I found a fire escape but it had a retractable ladder and you had to be on the second floor to release it.

Parked in the alley was a truck. I remembered the mailman telling me that the movers' truck was always parked there. As I walked toward it, I looked up at the second floor to see if I could figure out which was the alley window for office number 2002.

I was right behind the truck when I heard a window open. I ducked down so as not to be seen in case anyone looked out. I heard someone clear his throat and then spit out the window.

I pulled my head in a little farther. A second later the spit hit the pavement five feet away and then the window closed.

As I crouched there I found myself looking at the truck's rear stoplight. The red glass reflector had been broken, and there was only one small piece left attached to the rim, a long V-shaped sliver. I reached over, broke it off and put it in my jacket pocket.

I went around to the front of the building, entered the lobby and waited for the elevator. As it approached I heard people talking inside. When the door opened, I turned half away, pretending to be studying the building directory, and out of the corner of my eye watched the people who got off. I didn't recognize any of them. I got on the elevator and pushed the button for the third floor. I planned to get off there and walk down to two. The elevator started up and when it reached the second floor it stopped and the door opened. Directly opposite was the office of the Kowalski Brothers. I didn't know whether to dash out of the elevator before someone came from the office, or wait for the elevator door to close. I stood there immobilized. The wait seemed interminable. I wondered if the elevator was stuck. Then something clicked and the elevator door began slowly to slide shut, but the office door opened at that moment and the man with the bushy eyebrows and hazel-yellow eyes— Nick Kowalski—was staring at me with a startled expression on his face.

"Hey!" he said. He dashed toward the closing elevator and at the same time shouted for help. "Uncle Louie!"

Behind him a short barrel-chested man with a cigar in his mouth came to out of the office. He was wearing a gray suit, a navy-blue shirt and a white silk tie.

The elevator had an inner and an outer door. The outer door sealed off the elevator shaft from the hallway, and the inner one belonged to the elevator cab. Nick Kowalski did not manage to get his hand through to the inner door but he held the outer one open a few inches and apparently this prevented the elevator from moving.

142

Both doors were still open about two inches, and I watched as the uncle rushed out of the office. His hand was reaching inside his jacket to the armpit and when he took his hand out he was holding a pistol.

"Not here!" Nick screamed at his uncle. "Help me pull this door open."

I pounded Nick's hand with my fist. He lost his grip, the door slid shut and the elevator began to move, but it stopped abruptly after rising about three feet. They must have begun to pry open the outside door again, causing the safety mechanism to stop the elevator. Through the slit of the outside door, they began to force open the inner door. They managed about three inches. Ripping my shoe off, I smashed at the fingers around the door and it slid shut again. Still the elevator did not move; they must have been holding the outside door open. I noticed blood on the heel of my shoe.

They were talking outside. "Uncle Louie! Run up to the third floor and push the button. Shout down the shaft and I'll let the elevator go up."

I heard running footsteps. I studied the inside of the elevator. In the ceiling was a two-foot-square opening used by repairmen to get to the cable. A thin metal sheet lay over the opening. I jumped up and touched it and it slid a few inches to the side. I jumped up again and caught hold of the edge of the opening. Pulling myself partway into the hole in the elevator ceiling, I pushed the metal sheet aside with my body, got through the hole and stood on top of the elevator. I heard Nick's uncle shout down from the third floor: "Okay. Let go."

The elevator began to rise. I replaced the metal sheet over the hole. Beside me the cables were moving. The elevator reached the third floor and the doors opened. I heard Nick's uncle come into the elevator.

"What the . . . ?"

A moment later I heard Nick run up.

"He's not *here*," said the uncle.

Standing on top of the cab, I could reach the outside elevator

143

door at the fourth-floor level. I tried to force it open.

"Up *there*," I heard Nick say. Then someone jumped up and pushed the metal sheet to one side. Nick Kowalski and his uncle were standing in the elevator looking up through the hole. Nick jumped, caught the edge of the opening with his hands and held on, trying to pull himself up. I stepped on his fingers.

"Ow!"

He dropped, stumbling against his uncle. I succeeded in pushing open the fourth-floor elevator door about four inches. But I needed to open it farther and also to climb up about four feet to get out. I managed another five inches.

"Push the button for six," said Nick. "He wants to stay up there, we'll mash him against the top of the elevator shaft."

I looked down and saw the uncle push the button for the sixth floor. But because I had the door partly open on the fourth floor, the safety mechanism prevented the elevator from moving. Nick jumped up again and caught hold of my pants cuff with one hand. In trying to shake him off, I lost my hold on the fourth-floor door and it slipped shut. The cab began to rise. I stepped on Nick's fingers again and he dropped.

The elevator was rising now toward the top of the shaft. I wasn't sure if there would be enough space to prevent me from being crushed. I thought there would be, and knew that if these men had killed Smedlo they would not hesitate to kill me. As the elevator approached the top of the shaft, a loop of cable came rolling down past my face. Intellectually I still believed that there would probably be enough room for me to stay where I was, but I was overcome by the nightmarish fear of being crushed and at the last minute I dropped down through the hole into the hands of two men I felt sure would try to kill me, but not until later.

I knew I couldn't fight them so I didn't try. The uncle grabbed my arms and pinned them behind my back. They didn't seem to notice I wasn't struggling. I watched as Nick drew back his fist—the knuckles and fingers were bloody from being stepped

on and smashed by my shoe—and rammed it into my mouth.
I had once intentionally broken the handle off a teacup with my
fingers and when Nick's fist hit my mouth one of my front teeth
broke off with the same *crack!* sound. I tasted warm salty blood.
The punch also jarred my head and I felt dizzy. Everything was
dim, but I could see that the punch to my mouth had further
injured Nick's hand. Apparently the breaking tooth had given
him a very bad cut on the knuckles. A steady stream of blood
was coming from his hand. The elevator doors opened on the
sixth floor and they dragged me out.

"Down the back stairs to the office," said Nick. They shoved
me down four flights of stairs. The uncle held my arms while
Nick looked out into the hall on the second floor to make sure
no one was coming. Then they pushed me into their office.

The uncle slammed me into a chair. It was clear they didn't
know exactly what to do next, and neither did I. I felt my lip
with my tongue and found that blood was running down my
chin and dropping onto my jacket and pants. My first thought
was that I wouldn't be able to go outside with all that blood on
my suit. My second thought was that I was wearing only one
shoe. Somehow I had lost the other one after I smashed Nick's
hand with it.

"Look at your pants," said the uncle to Nick.

Nick's hand was bleeding profusely and the blood was dropping onto his pants. Nick glared at me with the most intense
look of hatred I had ever seen. He picked up a dictionary from
the desk and tried to hit me in the face with it. I turned my head
and the book glanced across the side of my face and stung my
ear. Nick grabbed my chin to keep me from turning away. An
instant before the second blow, I thought, I hope he doesn't
break another tooth. The odds were that before the day was
over I would be dead, but now all I could think of was how much
I dislike visiting the obnoxious little man who takes care of my
teeth.

When I regained consciousness, I found myself tied in the chair with a rag stuffed in my mouth.

"What the hell is keeping Mike?" the uncle was saying. "He only had nine banks in Staten Island."

"I told you three times, Uncle Louie," said Nick. "Dad had the last fifteen banks in Manhattan to do too."

"I hope nothing happened to him," said the uncle.

"Will you shut up, Uncle Louie? You're beginning to make *me* nervous."

The desk in the office was covered with small piles of money, mostly bills in large denominations. Nick picked up several lists, examined them and made some notations on a piece of paper.

"We have seven hundred and fifty-three thousand on this table, Uncle Louie. If Dad made all the banks on his list, he'll have another eighty-five thousand. That'll leave ten more banks in Manhattan, eight in Brooklyn, eight in the Bronx and three in Queens."

"The wise guy is awake," said the uncle, referring to me.

"Don't worry about him," said Nick. "Before we go we'll work him over and throw him down the elevator shaft."

He looked at his knuckles, which were now wrapped in a white handkerchief. My mind cleared very quickly. I was beginning to understand everything. The Kowalski brothers and the son, Nick Kowalski, had received the missing welfare checks. All those bank accounts had been opened so that a few checks could be deposited in each one without arousing suspicion. After the checks cleared the banks, the Kowalskis went around to each bank and drew out most of the money in cash. Months later, when the Welfare Department finally got around to notifying the banks about which checks were stolen, the banks would follow their normal procedure, which had worked in the past—they would try to subtract the amount of the stolen checks from each customer's balance. But in this case, each bank branch would find a customer at 126 Schermerhorn Street who had only a few dollars in his account, and correspondence from the bank would come back marked "Whereabouts un-known." The Kowalskis would be in South America or some-place with three-quarters of a million American dollars in cash.

I knew Smedlo had handled the missing checks because he still had had three in his pocket from the alphabetical list when he was killed. I was fairly sure Smedlo had arranged with Nolan from the main welfare office to remove the checks. Smedlo and Nolan had gone to school together and Nolan was one of Smed-lo's few friends, judging from the autographs in Smedlo's col-lege yearbook. Nolan was obviously covering up something or he wouldn't have denied knowing Smedlo when I first spoke to him.

Nolan had found a way to get the welfare checks out of the post office bags while they were in the back of the truck being delivered. It would have been simple for him to get into Dom-brow's desk after work some night and have duplicate keys made for each mailbag. Apparently he pulled out a prewrapped bundle of twenty checks from each bag, which would explain why the missing checks were in alphabetical order. Nolan may not even have known exactly how Smedlo was going to dispose of the checks. My hunch was that Smedlo had been killed be-cause he had been the only one who could link the stolen checks to the Kowalskis. Until I came along.

The office door opened and another man entered, an older version of Uncle Louie.

"Jesus, Mike, what kept you?" said Louie.

"We gotta get out of here fast," said the man.

"What's wrong, Dad?" said Nick Kowalski. "Where's your briefcase?"

"Who the hell is that?" said Nick's father, nodding toward me.

"Some wise guy trying to mess us up," said Uncle Louie. "Where's your briefcase, Mike? Where's the money?"

"I got robbed in the elevator. A nigger put a pistol in my back and got the whole fucking thing. Seventy-two thousand dollars plus my gun. The guy looked like a queer to me from the way he walked. Dressed like a queer too—red golf cap and yellow pants."

"This is getting ridiculous," said Nick. "First this creep, then a nigger. It's time to blow before somebody else tries to get into the act. Help me pack this money."

He opened his briefcase and put it on the desk. Suddenly there was a *bang!* and the opaque glass in the top half of the office door exploded into the room in a thousand fragments, like bird shot fired from a shotgun. Someone outside in the hall had fired a gun through the window. Three more shots ripped through the wood on the bottom of the door and the door began to swing slowly open. One of the shots had smashed a window opposite the door, another had sent a metal wastebasket skittering across the floor and the third had hit me in the calf of the leg.

Pat McCann stepped into the room with a smoking pistol in one hand and my shoe in the other. He raised the pistol, fired two shots into the ceiling, bringing down two chunks of plaster, and shouted, "Everybody freeze!" Then he pointed the gun at the Kowalskis. Uncle Louie made a very slight motion with his shoulder.

"I said *freeze!*" Pat screamed, and menaced him with the gun. Louie froze. The three of them seemed stunned by the shooting.

"Jesus, Ross," said Pat when he saw my battered face. He took the rag out of my mouth and untied me. "Can you make it over there and search them for guns?"

"I don't think so, Pat," I said, "I've got a bullet in my leg."

Pat looked back at the Kowalskis and his lip curled up in a combination of snarl and sneer.

"You crummy creeps," he said. "I oughta shoot *you* in the leg. It looks like I got here just in time."

I didn't have the heart to tell Pat that *he* had shot me in the leg, and there was no point in telling him that he had already fired six shots and therefore had nothing left in his pistol to shoot the Kowalskis with.

"You hold the gun, Ross," he said. He came over and handed it to me. "If one of these creeps moves an inch, don't aim for the leg. Blow his damn head off."

"I will," I said. I tried to put a vengeful, threatening look on my face to compensate for the lack of ammunition in the pistol. Pat walked around behind Louie Kowalski and took the gun from his shoulder holster, at which point I began to breathe a little easier. He found another gun in Louie's side pocket. Nick's father didn't have a gun. Nick had no gun either. Apparently he was the brains of the operation. He began to use them.

"Listen," he said. "I don't know who you guys are, and I don't care. There's plenty here for all of us. There's seven hundred and fifty thousand dollars on that table."

"Seven hundred and fifty or a thousand!" said Pat contemptuously. He had misunderstood the amount of money mentioned by Nick Kowalski.

"I said three-quarters of a million," said Nick.

"Bullshit," said Pat.

Seven hundred and fifty dollars was too petty to be considered; three-quarters of a million was too fantastic to be imagined.

"Pat, let me use one of the guns," I said, hoping to change the subject. "Yours must be almost out of ammunition."

Pat came over and gave me a gun. He picked up a thousand-dollar bill from the table. "What is this, Ross—fake money?"

"Not exactly, Pat. But let's talk about it later. Tie the Kowalskis up while I try to get Cooper and the assistant district attorney and Lieutenant Gregoria down here. Maybe they'll keep each other honest when they count the money."

I knew if I didn't call right away, I might begin to get ideas about the money myself. I picked up the phone and dialed.

twenty-five

"I'M TIRED of these games," said Cooper as he burst in the door with O'Toole, the dyspeptic, red-faced assistant district attorney who had directed the welfare check raid. Cooper saw the condition of my face. He looked at the Kowalskis, who were tied into chairs.

"You've been *fighting* again too," he said. "A million dollars in welfare checks is missing, the mayor's on our back, and you can't even bust one blind old lady."

"First of all, you petty, posturing, bureaucratic little flunky, I quit," I said. "Second, most of the million dollars is in that briefcase. We counted. Seven hundred and fifty-two thousand dollars. The rest of the money from those checks is still in about thirty banks. Except for seventy-two thousand dollars stolen by a Negro homosexual in a red golf cap and bright yellow slacks."

I hadn't decided yet whether to tell anyone that the Negro man was Valjean Wilcox.

I heard a siren in the distance and assumed it was the ambulance I had called to take me to the hospital.

"If you, or the mayor, or anyone else wants to know how all that money got in that briefcase, you can get the details from me at Mount Sinai Hospital—but don't come without champagne. French champagne. Lots of it. It's the first time I've been shot and I want to celebrate."

"Listen, Franklin—" said Cooper, but I cut him off.

"I'm serious, Cooper. With champagne, and a little courtesy, you might get a few more details."

The sound of a siren was right outside the building. Then it stopped abruptly and a moment later two patrolmen looked in the door.

"You people know anything about all that blood in the elevator? We got a complaint."

"This is the place," I said.

I could hear another siren in the distance. I hoped it was the ambulance. My leg was beginning to throb with pain.

"One of the men tied up over there killed Roy Smedlo, the welfare investigator who was killed in the Fifty-first Precinct," I said to the patrolmen. "Probably with this gun." I held up Louie's gun. "A homicide lieutenant—Gregoria—is on his way over. Tell him Smedlo was killed in the truck outside."

Again a siren was blaring outside the building. It stopped and in a moment Gregoria came in the door. From far away I heard the wail of another siren. I was beginning to feel the symptoms of shock. I was sweating but felt extremely cold and had a terrible headache.

"Lieutenant," I said, "one of those men that are tied up over there killed Smedlo. Check out this thirty-eight." I laid Louie's pistol on the desk. "It's probably the weapon. Or the one Pat McCann has. The truck they used is parked in the alley. The pieces of reflector light that Bumpy has are from the broken taillight on the truck. I have the piece that's missing. If Bumpy isn't out of jail today, I'm going to send the missing piece of reflector to the *Daily News* with a long letter."

"What the hell are you talking about?" said Gregoria.

The third siren was outside the building now.

"Uh uh uh, lieutenant," I said. "The same rules for you as for everyone else. If you need more information, I'll be at Mount Sinai Hospital. Bring champagne."

Two men in white pants and jackets appeared at the door with a stretcher.

151

"Who's Ross Franklin?" said one of them.

"I am," I said.

"You have Blue Cross coverage?" said the man.

"Yes," I said.

"What's the policy number?" said the other man. He had a form in his hand.

"Oh one four two six two nine five two," I said.

"Okay, Mr. Franklin, just lie down here."

"Good-bye, everyone," I said, and they wheeled me away.

twenty-six

PAUL GREGORIA—we were all on a first-name basis now—popped the cork of another champagne bottle.

"Who's ready for more?" he asked. "You, Ross?"

"Thanks," I said. "Could you crank this bed up a little, Horace?" I said.

"Sure, Ross," said Horace Cooper. He cranked up my hospital bed.

"More champagne, Horace?" said Paul.

"Thanks, Paul," said Horace.

"Tell us again how you came in shooting, Pat," said Mike O'Toole, the assistant district attorney.

"Well," said Pat, "I knew from Ross's friend Roberta at the welfare center that Ross had gone to the office of the movers. When I got there, I took the elevator up to three, so I could walk down without being seen. The elevator was smeared with blood, and there was this bloody shoe."

"By the way," I said, "where is that shoe?"

"You won't need it for at least a month," said Horace Cooper.

They were all so far gone on champagne that they laughed uproariously. My leg and foot were in a cast—suitably autographed by now—and the cast had to stay on for a month. I was able to restrain myself from joining in the laughter.

"I recognized that it was Ross's shoe because it was a black shoe with a brown shoelace, and I had given him a brown shoelace last Thursday when his broke. I got off on the third floor and the stairway down to the second floor was also smeared with blood. I listened outside the door of the movers' and when I heard them say they were gonna throw him down the elevator shaft I came in with my gun blazing."

I took another sip of champagne to try to ease a new twinge of pain in my leg. Finally the anesthetic effects of the champagne set in. The happy, laughing voices of Mike and Paul and Horace and Pat faded in my ears and I fell into a deep, dreamful sleep.

twenty-seven

I WAS SITTING with Roberta in her living room, looking out onto
Riverside Park and the Jersey shore across the Hudson River.
My leg was propped up on a chair. I was able to move around
with the aid of crutches. After a long night's sleep and a breakfast of steak, funnel cakes and champagne left over from the
hospital, I felt much better. My leg was extremely painful, but
my morale was good.

The Welfare Department had agreed to keep one welfare
case open for Maybell Brown, the blind woman. I was going to
stay on my job with Box 100, at least for a little while, and even
get something called a "meritorious increase" in pay. There was
a chance I might even get my picture in the *Daily News* again.
Roberta was going to take a few days off from work and nurse
me back to health. I planned to roast a pig on Friday.

The phone rang.

"Let it ring," I told Roberta.

"No one knows you're here, do they?" said Roberta.

"I don't think so. But they know you're here."

The phone rang about fifteen times and then stopped.
Roberta moved a little closer to me on the couch and we kissed.
Then the phone rang again. Roberta picked it up after the first
ring.

"It's for you," she said. I took the receiver.

"Ross?" said the voice at the other end. It was Valjean Wilcox.

"Where are you, Valjean?" I said.

"Let's just say Tito and I are in a warm climate."

"You have Tito?" I said.

"Of course. I told you I wanted a baby. I gave your adoption agencies eleven months to get me one. I didn't want to wait any longer. Willette signed legal papers giving Tito to me. And Smedlo's mother signed papers. She was so happy to get rid of the kid she wanted to pack me a lunch to take with me."

"You also have seventy-two thousand dollars that belongs to the New York City Welfare Department," I said.

"The way I look at that, Ross, the Welfare Department pays eight thousand dollars a year to keep kids like Tito in institutions. Eight thousand dollars a year times eighteen years is a hundred forty-four thousand dollars—did I do the math right, Ross?"

"I think so," I said.

"So I figure I'm saving the city money. I'll never ask them for another penny. And Tito's already seen *two* oceans. I showed him the Atlantic from the plane. Now he's looking at the Pacific."

"Right on, Valjean," I said.

"You really mean that, Ross?"

"Yes," I said.

She sent the sound of a kiss over the wire to me.

"Be careful, Valjean."

"I intend to be."

"Send me a postcard once in a while."

"I will," she said. She hung up.

Roberta looked at me. "She was in on the theft of those checks?" said Roberta.

"No," I said. "I was just fooling around with her." I didn't want anyone but me to know that Valjean was the man in the red cap.

156

The phone rang again and Roberta answered it.

"Hello," she said. She listened a moment. "Lori," she said, "does Daddy know you're calling me long distance?" She listened. "He is? Well, where's Mummy? . . . Don't cry, honey. I'll call your Uncle John at work and I'm sure he'll come right over, and I'll be out there before supper, I promise. You can't cry, Lori, because you have to help Ariel and Peter until Uncle John gets there. . . . That's the girl. Now as soon as I reach your Uncle John, I'll call you right back. Don't worry about anything. It'll be all right. Give my love to Ariel and Peter and tell them I'm coming to supper. Okay, dear, I'll call you back in five minutes."

Tears were running down her cheeks as she hung up.

"Those poor darlings," she said. "They behave so much better than adults."

"Your grandchildren?" I said.

"Yes," she said. "Mummy's gone away and Daddy's been crying in the bathroom for the last five hours and won't come out. I've got to get out there."

She called Uncle John, her daughter-in-law's brother, then called her granddaughter back. Then, while I phoned Kennedy Airport and made reservations for a noon flight to California, she packed.

I went out to the airport with her in a taxi.

"I'll call you tonight, if I can, or tomorrow morning," she said. "I might have to stay out there a good while. It sounds serious and their Uncle John is about as much help as a sponge rubber crutch, and I do mean sponge. He needs help himself."

"Are you sure you don't want me to come with you?"

"Absolutely."

I realized that with my leg in a cast I wouldn't be much help to anyone.

Airports always make me sad and we both cried when we kissed good-bye.

twenty-eight

FROM THE AIRPORT I took a cab to 119 Herzl Street. Bumpy Jackson was on the front stoop with Willamae Jones' son Gabriel. Bumpy was fixing up Gabriel's Afro hairdo.

"Hey, bro," he said when he saw me.

"Hi!" said Gabriel, and gave me a clenched-fist salute.

"You taught him the black power salute?" I said to Bumpy somewhat reproachfully.

"You a nice man," said Bumpy, "but you sorta square in a lot of ways. That ain't no black power salute. I seen a white boy on Johnny Carson give that salute to the audience, man. No jive. It just means 'Right on.' It means 'You do your thing, baby—and I'll do mine.' "

"Oh," I said.

"What happened to your leg?" said Bumpy.

"I got shot," I said. "By one of my own men."

"They the most dangerous," said Bumpy. "I ought to know."

"In my case it was an accident," I said.

"Don't be too sure," said Bumpy. "That's what they claimed in my case too."

"You seem to be in a good mood," I said.

"Why shouldn't I be. If my lawsuit comes in, I'll have some real pocket money, not just my little disability check."

"What lawsuit?"

"Jackson versus the police commissioner."

"What kind of a suit?" I said.

"False arrest."

"Well, Bumpy," I said, "I don't see how you can make that stick. Gregoria was mistaken when he arrested you, but he did have some evidence. There's a difference between a mistake and false arrest."

"Suppose they know you didn't do it, they just arrest you to throw the real killer off balance, make him overconfident?"

"Come on, Bumpy," I said. "Gregoria didn't have the slightest idea that the Kowalskis killed Smedlo. He never even heard of the Kowalskis until I told him about them."

Bumpy picked up a copy of the *Daily News*, opened it to an inside page and read aloud from the story:

" 'Jackson was never a serious suspect,' said Homicide Lieutenant Paul Gregoria. Gregoria broke the case on Tuesday morning when he arrested the alleged killers with three-quarters of a million dollars in cash in their possession. 'If the Kowalskis did not realize they were under suspicion, I believed they would expose themselves, and they did,' Gregoria told newsmen."

"That's bullshit," I said.

"It's the kind of bullshit that could cost the city a nice lump sum settlement on a false arrest case. I got a real smart young antipoverty lawyer gonna take the case for me. He's drawing up the papers right now. I figure they owe me something. No matter how you look at it, it wasn't right what they done to me. I didn't show it, man, but bein' in that jail really put me *down*. I dreamed about the electric chair. I woke up screamin' twice."

"Bumpy, they don't have the electric chair in New York anymore."

"Well, no one told *me* that, man. What do they use now—a firing squad?"

"There's no death penalty, Bumpy."

"Well, I can't say I agree with that either. You kill another human being, man, you oughta pay for it."

"Well, anyway, Bumpy, I just stopped by to check things out."

"Heard anything from Valjean?" he asked.

"I got a call from her. She's all right."

"Where is she?" said Bumpy.

"She didn't say."

"Well, things work out," said Bumpy. "She always did love that kid. She lost a baby herself, you know, about the time Tito was born."

"No," I said. "I didn't know."

"Yeah," said Bumpy. "I don't know the whole story."

"Well, you never do," I said.

"That's true," said Bumpy. "Now take this story in the *News*." He folded the paper back to page 3 and showed me a headline: "EX MENTAL PATIENT STABBED."

There was a picture of a man in handcuffs being led away by two policemen. I read the caption of the picture. "Joseph Castori of 205 W. 71st St. is led away by police after allegedly stabbing Mildred Hummock, an ex-mental patient, in the eyes with a penknife."

I glanced at the body of the story.

"I complained about her but nobody paid attention so I took the law into my own hands," said Castori, an unemployed laborer.

"Now there's more to *that* story which they ain't printin'," said Bumpy. "A man don't do a thing like that for no reason."

"You're right," I said. "Well, I have to be going. If I can ever help you out with anything, just send a letter to Box 100."

"Okay, bro. I appreciate what you done already."

I walked down Herzl. On my left were the smashed automobiles sitting on their axles in front of the one-family homes. On my right was the vacant, garbage-filled lot and then the abandoned building where Mrs. Procacino lived.

I thought of Mrs. Smedlo. "I'm not prejudiced. I rent the

160

second floor to an Italian family." I thought of Roy Smedlo. "Don't push me, Franklin. You don't play in my league. You could get *hurt!*" I thought of Mrs. Harm's linoleum money deposited in Smedlo's bank account. I thought of Smedlo's case records: "This is not a serious suicide threat. Miss Perez is constantly making this threat but never follows through." I thought of the little girls in the subway. I thought of Roberta's plane moving down the runway.

I walked past the rubble-strewn lot with the Model Cities sign dangling from the fence.

I decided to get on the subway and go down to my office. What I really needed to cheer me up was to read a big batch of new letters to Box 100.